Happy New ~~Year~~ ... One resolution th~~e readers of Presents~~ like to keep is making time just for themselves by curling up with their favorite books and escaping into a world of glamour, passion and seduction! So why not try this for yourselves, and pick up a Harlequin Presents today?

We've got a great selection for you this month, with THE ROYAL HOUSE OF NIROLI series leading the way. In *Bride by Royal Appointment* by Raye Morgan, Adam must put aside his royal revenge to marry Elena. Then, favorite author Lynne Graham will start your New Year with a bang, with *The Desert Sheikh's Captive Wife*, the first part in her trilogy THE RICH, THE RUTHLESS AND THE REALLY HANDSOME. Jacqueline Baird brings you a brooding Italian seducing his ex-wife in *The Italian Billionaire's Ruthless Revenge*, while in *Bought for Her Baby* by Melanie Milburne, there's a gorgeous Greek claiming a mistress! *The Frenchman's Marriage Demand* by Chantelle Shaw has a sexy millionaire furious that Freya's claiming he has a child, and in *The Virgin's Wedding Night* by Sara Craven, an innocent woman has no choice but to turn to a smoldering Greek for a marriage of convenience. Lee Wilkinson brings you a tycoon holding the key to Sophia's precious secret in *The Padova Pearls*, and, finally, in *The Italian's Chosen Wife* by fantastic new author Kate Hewitt, Italy's most notorious tycoon chooses a waitress to be his bride!

Dinner at 8

Don't be late!

He's suave and sophisticated.

He's undeniably charming.

And, above all, he treats her like a lady….

But beneath the tux, there's a primal, passionate lover who's determined to make her his!

Wined, dined and swept away by a British billionaire!

Lee Wilkinson

THE PADOVA PEARLS

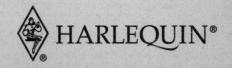

TORONTO • NEW YORK • LONDON
AMSTERDAM • PARIS • SYDNEY • HAMBURG
STOCKHOLM • ATHENS • TOKYO • MILAN • MADRID
PRAGUE • WARSAW • BUDAPEST • AUCKLAND

ISBN-13: 978-0-373-12697-2
ISBN-10:   0-373-12697-2

THE PADOVA PEARLS

First North American Publication 2008.

www.eHarlequin.com

Printed in U.S.A.

All about the author...
Lee Wilkinson

LEE WILKINSON attended an all-girls school, where her teachers, often finding her daydreaming, declared that she "lived inside her own head." That is still largely true today. Until her marriage, she had a variety of jobs, ranging from a departmental manager to modeling swimsuits and underwear.

An only child and an avid reader from an early age, she began writing when she, her husband and their two children moved to Derbyshire. She started with short stories and magazine serials before going on to write romances for Harlequin.

Lee is a lover of animals, and after losing Kelly, her adored German shepherd, she adopted a rescue dog named Thorn, who looks like a pit bull and acts like a big softy, apart from when the postman calls. Then he has to be restrained, otherwise he goes berserk and shreds the mail.

Traveling has always been one of Lee's main pleasures. After crossing Australia and America in a motor home, and traveling round the world on two separate occasions, she still, periodically, suffers from itchy feet.

She enjoys walking and cooking, log fires and red wine, music and the theater, and still much prefers books to television—both reading and writing them.

CHAPTER ONE

THE early June evening was damp and overcast, prematurely dark. Sophia Jordan, a plastic carrier bag in her hand, a stone-coloured mac belted round her slim waist, was hurrying home. Back to the ground floor flat in Roleston Square, Belgravia, she had shared with her late father, Peter.

The thought of the empty flat still filled her with sadness for though her father had been quite ill for the past year, his death, some twelve weeks earlier, had in the end been sudden and un-expected and had left her bereft and lonely.

Old Mrs Caldwell, a widow who owned the large house in Roleston Square and, along with her niece, Eva, occupied the flat across the hallway, had understood how she felt and been very kind.

Just that morning when Sophia had knocked at her door to enquire what shopping she needed, grey-haired and stooped, cheerful in spite of her arthritis, the old lady had urged, 'Come across after work, dearie, and we'll have some supper together.

'Though with Eva being away on that special course,' she had added, 'I'm afraid you'll have to do the cooking, if you don't mind?'

'Of course I don't mind. Is there anything in particular you'd like me to cook?'

'Would it be any trouble to make a paella?'

Stooping to stroke the marmalade cat that was winding sinuously around her ankles, Sophia said, 'No trouble at all.'

'Wonderful!' the old lady had cried enthusiastically. 'I haven't had a paella since Arthur took me to Spain on holiday. Eva dislikes all rice dishes.'

'Then I'll do the shopping on my way home tonight, and pop across as soon as I've changed.'

Looking delighted, Mrs Caldwell had promised, 'I'll have the table set ready.'

Handing Sophia a list and some money, she'd added, 'It'll be lovely to have your company *and* a freshly cooked meal.'

On hearing about Sophia's plans for the evening, David Renton, international art dealer and owner of A Volonté, the prestigious gallery where she worked, had suggested, 'Why don't you leave half an hour early? Joanna can cope, and you've put in a great deal of extra time over your father's exhibition.'

Peter Jordan had been a very talented amateur painter and after his death, David—his long time friend—had remarked, 'His work is brilliant. It's a pity he was too modest to agree to me showing it.

'I tried to persuade him by telling him that seeing his canvases would inspire other young amateur painters. But he still held back.'

'I really think he was coming round to your way of thinking,' Sophia had said. 'He was talking about it a few days before he died.'

'Then why don't we put on an exhibition of his work as a kind of memorial? A celebration of his life? If we include his miniatures, there should be enough to fill the balcony.'

Liking the idea, Sophia had agreed.

She had collected together all her father's paintings, except for a single canvas that hung in her bedroom.

It was a head and shoulders portrait of a handsome young man with fair hair and dark eyes, and a mouth that, with its combination of asceticism and sensuality, had always affected her strongly.

Since her childhood, the portrait had held a strange fascination for her, and as a teenager she had woven extravagantly romantic dreams around it.

Knowing how much she liked it, her father had given it to her for her sixteenth birthday.

His pleasure had been in the actual painting and, with little regard for his own talent, he had often given the finished portrait to his sitter. Which meant that there weren't all that many for a lifetime's work.

However, David had collected what there were and taken them over to the gallery.

There, Sophia had worked long hours to hang them, produce catalogues and organize the advance publicity. Now the one-man exhibition was ready and due to open the following morning.

That off her mind, she had accepted David's kind offer and left the gallery at six-thirty, stopping at the local store to do the necessary shopping.

It was Friday night and the store was crowded. By the time she had succeeded in battling her way through an obstacle course of people and trolleys, one of her stockings was laddered and her heavy coil of hair was coming down.

Bundling it up again, she felt for the clip that held it in place, only to find it was missing.

The queue at the checkout was a long one and on leaving the store she found a fine drizzle had started to fall.

With an exasperated sigh, she turned up the collar of her mac and tucked the dark silky mass of hair into it as best she could.

Only when she was walking away from the 'convenience' store did she appreciate wryly that it would have been a great deal more convenient if her purchases, which included milk and tinned food for Mrs Caldwell's three cats, had been put into two carriers rather than one.

As it was, she had to keep swapping the heavy bag from hand to hand as the thin plastic handles cut into her fingers, stopping the blood flow.

She was changing hands for the umpteenth time when one of the flimsy handles gave way, letting the bag drop and spilling its contents at the feet of a tall, fair-haired man who was walking some half a dozen paces behind her.

While the other pedestrians parted and flowed smoothly either side, like water round a rock, the well-dressed stranger stooped and with deft efficiency began to gather all the items together.

As she stared down at his bent head, noticing how the thick blond hair, dampened by the drizzle, was trying to curl, he replaced the groceries in the carrier. As he picked up the last item he laughed, 'Good thing there's no eggs.'

His voice was pleasant and well-modulated, with a fascinating hint of an accent she couldn't quite place.

Holding the carrier to him with one arm, the other supporting the bottom, he rose to his feet, dwarfing her five foot seven.

Glancing up into his handsome face, she felt a jolt of recognition, a shock of surprise.

But while her brain insisted that it couldn't be *him*, her heart and eyes told her it was.

Though she was unable to make out the exact colour of his dark, long-lashed eyes, the strong, clear-cut features, the beautiful, ascetic mouth with its controlled upper lip and sensuous lower, the cleft chin and squarish jaw, were as familiar to her as her own face.

She was filled with joy and wonderment, an overriding sense of *fulfilment,* as though she had been subconsciously waiting for this meeting. As though it had been preordained.

As she stared at him, he went on, 'Oh dear, I'm very much

afraid that the whole thing's starting to tear open. Have you very far to go?'

Knocked off balance by the strangeness of it all, she stammered, 'N-no, not far. Just a little way down Roleston Road.'

Hitching the carrier a little higher, he suggested, 'Then suppose you lead on?'

Her natural good manners coming to the fore, she managed, 'Thank you, but I don't want to take you out of your way,' then waited in an agony of suspense. If he just handed over the shopping and walked away she would never see him again.

But, to her vast relief, he did no such thing.

With a little smile, he told her, 'As it happens I'm going in the same direction.'

The excitement of seeing *him*—only it couldn't possibly be *him*—and the sheer charm of that white, crooked smile sent her heart winging, making her forget, momentarily, the sadness that had been her constant companion over the last few weeks.

After a second or two, she said breathlessly, 'Well, if you're sure it's no trouble?'

'I'm sure.'

She returned his smile and, feeling as if something momentous had happened, tried to contain the fluttery excitement that was so unlike her.

As they began to walk on, the stranger—for in spite of that instant, joyful recognition she knew they had never met before—queried, 'So you live on Roleston Road?'

'No, just off, on Roleston Square. I've a flat in one of the old Georgian houses that overlook the Square's gardens.'

He raised a well-marked brow. 'You live alone?'

'I do now.'

'You're very young to live alone.'

'I'm not that young.'

Glancing at her lovely heart-shaped face with its flawless skin and almond eyes, the winged brows, the small straight nose and generous mouth, the long curly tendrils of seal-dark hair that had escaped from her collar, he said, 'You look about sixteen.'

'I'm twenty-five.'

'Twenty-five,' he repeated, as though the knowledge gave him some satisfaction. Then, harking back, 'So how long have you lived alone?'

Her voice wasn't quite steady as, with remembered grief, she told him, 'Since my father died a few months ago.'

He caught the sadness in her tone and asked, 'Was it unexpected?'

'In a way. He'd been ill for quite a long time, but in the end it was sudden.' Sophia could feel a tear begin to form but quickly brushed it away.

He probed gently, 'And your mother?'

'She died when I was about seven.'

'Any brothers or sisters?'

'No. I was an only child.'

He frowned a little. 'Your father couldn't have been very old?'

Sophia shook her head. 'Dad was just sixty-two. He didn't marry until he was thirty-six.'

'And after your mother died he didn't remarry?' he questioned.

'No.' She shook her head again. 'I've never understood why. Apart from the fact that he was good-looking and talented, he was kind and thoughtful, a really nice person with a wonderful sense of humour…'

'In what way was he talented?'

'He painted.' Sophia smiled at the memory of her father's talent.

'It was his profession?'

'No. He was a diplomat. Painting had always been his hobby. But when, after his accident, he retired from the diplomatic service, he did a lot more.'

'Landscapes?'

'Some, but portraits mainly. He painted one that's very like you.'

He gave her a quizzical glance and, embarrassed, she wondered what on earth had made her blurt that out. Except that it was the simple truth.

'Very like me?' He sounded amused.

'Yes.'

'Really? And is his work good?'

'I've heard it described as brilliant.'

Seeing a look on her companion's face that might have been scepticism, she added defensively, 'There's going to be an exhibition of his paintings at the art gallery where I work.'

'Which gallery is that?' he enquired politely.

'A Volonté.'

'Then you're an artist too?'

She shook her head. 'Though I wanted to be, and went to art school with that intention, unfortunately I don't have his talent.'

'What exactly do you do at the gallery?'

'As well as helping to sell pictures, I value them, set up exhibitions, take care of the photography and cataloguing and do any cleaning and restoring that may be necessary.'

Seeing her companion raise his eyebrows, she explained, 'Before I joined the gallery I spent two years working in a museum cleaning and restoring old or damaged paintings. I found I had a flair for it, and it was work I really enjoyed.'

'An invaluable skill.'

'Dad thought so.'

'You must miss him.'

'I do. Very much.' She swallowed past the lump in her throat. 'I still haven't got used to being on my own…' She let the words tail off as common sense shouldered its way in. Normally she was somewhat reserved, even with her friends, so why on earth was she opening her heart like this to a man she didn't know?

Only she *did* know him.

She had always known him.

'Surely there's a special boyfriend?'

'Not now. I was engaged to be married, but when Dad became worse and I didn't want to leave him alone in the evenings, it put a strain on the relationship. Philip resented the fact that I was no longer a free agent, and finally I gave him back his ring.'

'It must have been hard for you.'

'Not as hard as it might have been,' she admitted honestly. 'After he'd gone, I realized that, though I'd been fond of him, I hadn't really *loved* him.'

She had also realized that she'd only imagined herself in love because he'd reminded her a little of the man in her portrait.

'And there's been no one since?'

She shook her head.

With a grin, the stranger said, 'From the amount of shopping, I felt sure you must be feeding a small army of suitors.'

His teasing lightening the mood, she told him, 'It's for the old lady who owns the house and lives in the flat opposite. She's on her own at the moment and she's invited me to supper.'

'Any chance of her taking a rain check? I was about to ask you to have dinner with me.'

Sophia's heart leapt and then plummeted as she realized she couldn't accept his invitation.

It took a lot of willpower, but still she said, 'I'm sorry, but I can't let her down. She's really looking forward to the evening, and I've promised to do the cooking.'

'Pity.'

He said nothing further and she wondered if he had regretted his spur-of-the-moment invitation and been relieved when she'd refused.

But somehow she didn't think so.

They turned the corner into the quiet, tree-lined Square, its central gardens set with green lawns and bright flower-beds, and stopped outside the porticoed entrance of number twelve.

Yellow light from one ground floor window and the fanlight above the door was spilling across the pavement. But, as she might have expected, the upper windows were dark. The whole of the upstairs was one flat, and its tenants—a husband and wife team of lawyers who owned a boat and went sailing every weekend—would be gone.

Glancing at the lighted window, Sophia noticed one of the curtains move, and guessed that Mrs Caldwell had been looking out for her and seen them arrive.

As she fished in her handbag for her keys, hoping very much that the stranger would ask to see her some other time, she queried, 'Do you live in this area?'

'No. I don't live in London at all, I'm just here on business.'

'Oh.' Her heart sank.

Holding the carrier with one arm, he took the keys and, choosing the right one at his first attempt, opened the front door and held it wide for her.

As they crossed the hall, Mrs Caldwell appeared at her door. 'Oh, there you are, my dear!' she exclaimed. 'I was beginning to wonder if you'd been forced to work late.'

'I actually left early, but it took me rather a long time to do the shopping,' Sophia explained.

'Friday nights have always been busy,' Mrs Caldwell agreed. Then, glancing with interest at the tall, good-looking man by Sophia's side, she suggested, 'If you want to opt out of our arrangement and make other plans, I don't mind.'

Aware that the fair-haired stranger was waiting for her answer, after an almost imperceptible hesitation, Sophia said, 'No, of course I don't...'

Sensing that he was still staring at her, and wondering if he was annoyed because she hadn't taken advantage of the old lady's offer, she went on resolutely, 'I'll be over as soon as I've changed out of my suit.'

'There's no need to hurry, dearie. In the meantime I'll leave the door on the latch and pour us both a glass of sherry.' The old lady beamed at her and disappeared back inside.

Having opened Sophia's door and waited until she had switched on the lights, her companion followed her through the small lobby and into the pleasantly spacious combined living-room and kitchen.

While she took off her mac, he put the groceries carefully on the coffee table and, glancing around, remarked, 'I'm surprised to find it's open-plan.'

When he looked straight at her again, she could see that his eyes, like those of the portrait, were a clear grey and so dark they were almost charcoal. Eyes that were intriguingly at odds with his naturally fair hair.

Dragging her gaze away with an effort, she told him, 'When Mrs Caldwell had the house converted into three flats, she decided on extensive alterations.'

Nodding his head in approval, he said, 'I must say it works extremely well. It must be a pleasant place to live.'

'I've always liked it,' Sophia agreed. Then, anxious to know more about him, 'So where do you live?'

'Since I left university, I've been living mainly in New York.'

'Oh.' Did that mean he *still* lived in New York? If he did, that seemed to rule out any chance of getting to know him better.

Swamped by disappointment, she took a deep, steadying breath. Even so her voice was a little jerky as she said, 'I've been wondering about your accent… It doesn't seem typically American.'

'It isn't,' he admitted. 'It's a bit of a mixture. I was taken to live in the States as a child but, following a long family tradition, I went to university in England.'

'Then you have English roots?'

'On my father's side, but my mother's Italian.'

An Italian mother might well explain why he had olive-toned skin rather than being fair skinned like most natural blonds... And no doubt it accounted for that subtle and intriguing *difference* in his accent.

With a little stir of excitement that they had something in common, she remarked, 'My mother was Italian too.'

'An odd coincidence,' he observed smoothly. 'What was her name?'

'Maria.'

She waited for some further comment or question about her mother but, rather to her surprise, he changed the subject to ask, 'Will you be staying here now you're on your own?'

'I'm not sure. With three bedrooms, it's a lot bigger than I need. When Dad was alive it was ideal. He used the third bedroom, the one on the north side, as his studio.'

'That reminds me, do you still have that portrait? The one you said looks like me?'

'Yes.'

'If I may, I'd rather like to see it. You've succeeded in whetting my curiosity.'

Feeling distinctly awkward, she explained, 'It hangs in my bedroom.'

Looking into those beautiful eyes he could now see were a dark green, flecked with gold, he assured her with gentle mockery, 'I won't let that bother me, if you don't let it bother you.'

The simple fact that it did hang in her bedroom wouldn't have bothered her. What made her hesitate was that it was so *like* him, and it would be akin to baring her soul if he picked up how strongly she felt about it.

Noting her hesitation, he began carefully, 'If it *does* bother you—'

Pulling herself together, she assured him, 'No, no, of course it doesn't bother me.'

Looking unconvinced, he suggested, 'Perhaps you'd prefer to show me some of your father's other work?'

She shook her head. 'All the rest of Dad's paintings are over at the exhibition.'

'So why was that particular one left out?'

'Because it was never finished.' Making up her mind, she added, 'Come and take a look.'

Her heart racing uncomfortably fast, she ushered him along a wide corridor to her bedroom and, switching on the light, led the way inside.

It was simply furnished, with a dusky-pink carpet and off-white walls. The picture, the only one in the room, hung between the two windows.

Standing in front of it, the stranger stared at it in silence.

The column of the throat, the broad shoulders and the suggestion of an open-necked shirt, had been merely sketched in. But the well-shaped head, with its thick fair hair and neatly set ears, and the face, with its strong features and dark grey eyes beneath level brows, its beautiful mouth and cleft chin, was complete.

Glancing from one to the other, Sophie saw that the likeness between the portrait and the stranger was just as striking as she had imagined.

She felt a queer tug at her heart.

The only difference she could spot was that her companion's hair was somewhat shorter than that of the man in the portrait, and his brows and lashes were several shades darker.

Other than that, he *could* have been the sitter.

Only of course he *couldn't*.

It must have been painted either before he was born or when he was still a very young child.

After a moment or two of absolute stillness, the stranger said slowly, 'Surely this could have been put in the exhibition?'

It *could*. The simple truth was that she hadn't wanted to share it with anyone else. It would have been like other people being given access to a secret and very personal diary.

When she said nothing, he went on, 'Your father was a very fine artist. Those eyes are alive... And you're right about it being like me. I could be looking in a mirror. When did he paint it?'

'I'm not sure. Certainly before I was born. I've known it all my life.'

'Have you any idea who the sitter was?'

She shook her head. 'I'm afraid I haven't. I once asked my father, but he said, "Oh, just someone I met briefly a long time ago."'

'I see. Well, thank you for showing it to me.'

She was expecting him to say something further, to speculate on the likeness, remark on the coincidence, the strangeness of it all.

But he turned away and, noticing the box standing on her dressing table, commented, 'Your jewellery box is a lovely piece of work.'

'Yes, it was Dad's last gift to me. I found it hidden in his bureau.'

'Filled with priceless jewels, no doubt?' It was said quizzically, as though he'd recognized her sadness and was hoping to alleviate it.

She smiled. 'Empty, unfortunately.'

As she led him back to the living-room, he asked, 'When does your father's exhibition open?'

'Tomorrow morning, for a month. Though David—the

owner of the gallery—did say he would keep it open for as long as people kept coming in to see it.'

Then, sensing that he was about to go, and still hoping against hope that he might suggest seeing her again, she queried, 'How long are you in London for?'

Her last shred of hope vanished when he answered, 'I'm flying out tomorrow.'

Before she could think of anything else to say, he remarked with stunning finality, 'Well, I've taken up enough of your time. I guess I'd better go and let you get changed.'

Desperate to keep him, she began, 'I really can't thank you enough for your help…'

'It was my pleasure,' he said formally. 'Enjoy your evening. *Arrivederci*.'

As she stood stricken, the latch clicked behind him. A second or two later she heard the slam of the front door.

He was gone.

And she didn't even know his name.

Why, oh, why, had she let him walk out just like that?

Though what else could she have done?

She could have invited him to have supper with them. Mrs Caldwell wouldn't have minded, she felt sure, and there was more than enough food for three.

That way at least she would have had his company for an hour or two longer.

But she'd missed her chance. He was gone, and it was too late for regrets.

If only she had been free to have dinner with him. Though what could it have led to? If he *did* live in New York, there would have been little chance of seeing him again.

Still the nagging ache of disappointment, the futile longing for what might have been, the empty feeling of loss, persisted as she tried to make sense of the brief encounter.

Why had fate brought him into her life only to let him walk out again?

She felt as though she had been robbed of something infinitely precious, something that should have been rightfully hers…

Becoming aware that she was standing like a fool staring at the closed door and Mrs Caldwell would be waiting for her, Sophia pulled herself together and went to dry her hair and change.

Resisting the desire to stand and stare at the portrait, she swapped her business suit for a skirt and top and leaving her hair loose, hurried back to the living-room.

There, she quickly sorted out the old lady's change, picked up the carrier bag and glanced around for her keys.

They were nowhere to be seen.

But the stranger had actually opened the door, so he might have left them in the lock.

She took a quick look, but they weren't there.

So what had he done with them?

When another glance around failed to locate them, it occurred to her that he might well have dropped them into the carrier when he'd put the shopping down.

In that case she'd find them when she unpacked.

Taking the spare set of keys from the sideboard drawer, she switched off the light and, closing the door behind her, hurried across the hall.

As she approached the old lady's partly open door she could hear what sounded like one of the soaps on the television.

Calling, 'It's me,' she let herself in and went through to the living-room.

Like Sophia's own, the old lady's flat was light and spacious, with a combined living-room and kitchen. A long fire was throwing out a welcome warmth and two schooners of pale sherry were waiting on the coffee table.

Mrs Caldwell, who was standing by the window looking

through a chink in the curtains, turned to say, 'Do make yourself at home, dearie.'

Sophia put the old lady's change on the coffee table and, having crossed to the kitchen, began to unpack the shopping, while Sam, the boldest of the two marmalade kittens, rubbed against her leg, purring like a small traction engine.

Picking up the remote control, Mrs Caldwell switched off the television and, settling herself on the couch, urged, 'Why don't you sit down and drink your sherry before you start cooking?'

Aware that the old lady went to bed fairly early, Sophia suggested, 'It might make more sense to drink it while I'm getting the paella ready. That way we won't be too late having supper.'

'Perhaps you're right.'

Sophia unpacked the last of the groceries and, finding no trace of the missing keys, collected her glass of sherry.

While she sipped it, with swift efficiency she sliced onions, peppers and tomatoes, added a crushed clove of garlic and began to fry them lightly.

'The paella smells nice already,' Mrs Caldwell commented. 'I must say I'm starting to feel distinctly hungry.'

'In that case, I'm rather pleased I decided to buy most of the ingredients ready-cooked and make the quick version.'

'That was good thinking,' the old lady agreed. Then, eagerly, 'Who was the perfectly *gorgeous* young man who came in with you?'

Trying to sound casual, unconcerned, Sophia admitted, 'I'm afraid I've no idea.'

'But surely you know him?'

'No, not at all. He just offered to carry the shopping when one of the handles on the bag broke.'

Mrs Caldwell was clearly disappointed. 'Didn't you find out *anything* about him? Where he lives? What he does for a living?

Whether or not he has a steady girlfriend? I would have done at your age.'

Forced to smile, Sophia said, 'All I know is that he's in London on business… Oh, and that while his father has English roots, and he went to university in England, his mother comes from Italy.'

'Well, that's something you and he have in common. Oh, by the way, I've been meaning to ask you, have you still got relatives in Italy?'

'If I have they're distant ones. Like me, my mother was an only child, and her parents have been dead for quite a few years.'

'I wondered, because the man who came to see your father was Italian.'

Sophia was surprised. 'Someone visited Dad? How long ago?'

'Quite a while ago now,' Mrs Caldwell answered vaguely. 'Didn't he tell you?'

'No, this is the first I've heard of it.'

The old lady was obviously taken aback. 'That's peculiar… Well, this man arrived one day while you were at the gallery. He came in a taxi.'

'What was he like?'

'He was a good-looking man, short and thick-set, the same kind of build as my Arthur, with a thatch of white hair. He must have been somewhere in the region of sixty, but he looked younger because his eyebrows were still jet-black.

'He found your front door buzzer wasn't working properly and rang mine. When I answered, he explained to me in very poor English that he was looking for a Signor Jordan. He had a package for him.'

'What kind of package?' Sophia asked curiously.

'It was a parcel, about so big…' The old lady sketched the size in the air. 'I told him to go across the hall and ring the bell of your flat. Then I waited until I saw your father open the door and let him in.

'He only stayed a couple of minutes, then left in the same taxi that brought him.'

Sophia frowned. Why hadn't her father said anything about having a visitor? It was most unlike him. And, with so little happening in his life, he couldn't have *forgotten*…

'But, to get back to the young man who carried the shopping—' Mrs Caldwell broke into her thoughts '—I'm surprised he didn't ask you out.'

Stifling a sigh, Sophia remarked with determined lightness, 'I'm afraid we're just destined to be ships that pass in the night.'

'But you were attracted to him.' It was a statement, not a question.

Trying to dissemble, Sophia asked, 'What makes you think that?'

'Dearie, it was obvious.'

Feeling her colour rise, Sophia said, 'For all I know, he's married.'

She had judged him to be in his late twenties or early thirties, so it was odds-on that he was either married or in some kind of stable relationship.

Oh, surely not, when he'd invited her to have dinner with him…

But the fact that he'd asked her out didn't necessarily mean he was unattached. Perhaps if he travelled a lot he took his pleasure where he could find it…

'I happened to notice his left hand,' Mrs Caldwell told her. 'He wasn't wearing a ring.' With a sly glance, she added, 'It's high time you started to look for a husband.'

Sophia poured rice into a large cast-iron frying pan and began to stir in the stock. 'I don't know where to start looking.'

'You know what they say—love is where you find it. All it takes is mutual attraction to spark it off.' Then, thoughtfully,

'There was something about the way that young man looked at you that showed *he* was attracted. Very attracted.

'Oh, I know what you're thinking… I only got a quick glimpse of you both together. But that's all it takes. I felt sure he would ask you out. Perhaps tomorrow he'll—'

'He's going home tomorrow,' Sophia said flatly.

'That's a shame. One date might have been all that was needed to start a transatlantic courtship. An old-fashioned word, but a nice one, don't you think?'

Before Sophia could answer, she went on, 'It's a pity you didn't ask him to have supper with us.'

'I only thought about it after he'd gone. Of course he might not have accepted.'

'I rather fancy he would. When I heard the front door close, I looked out. He didn't just walk away, you know. He stood under that tree for several minutes watching your window. In fact he'd only just disappeared when you came over.'

Sophia was filled with disappointment. If only she'd looked out and seen him there, she might have plucked up the courage to go and issue an invitation.

But it seemed it wasn't to be.

CHAPTER TWO

PERHAPS Mrs Caldwell picked up that disappointment because she changed the subject by asking, 'Are you showing your father's miniatures?'

'Yes. There's plenty of space for them, and they're some of Dad's best work.'

'My favourite is the one of the dark-haired girl in that beautiful blue silk ball gown. She's wearing such exquisite pearls and holding what looks like a carnival mask... It always reminds me a little of you...'

Sophia knew the one she meant. It was another of her father's portraits that particularly appealed to her. Judging by the gown and the hairstyle, it had been copied from a much older painting.

But when she had asked him where he'd first seen the original, he had replied that it was so long ago he'd quite forgotten.

'When I mentioned to Peter how much I liked it,' the old lady went on, 'he told me that it was *his* favourite too...

'I miss him, you know,' she added abruptly. 'I enjoyed the games of cribbage we sometimes used to play in an afternoon.'

'I know he enjoyed them too.'

Her eyes suspiciously bright, Mrs Caldwell sat up straighter and demanded, 'So how is the exhibition coming along?'

'We're all set to open tomorrow morning.'

While the paella finished cooking they talked companionably about the exhibition in particular and painting in general.

When the meal was ready, Mrs Caldwell suggested frivolously, 'Let's have a bottle of wine. There's several in the rack. Make it a Rioja and we'll pretend we're in Spain.'

After they had toasted each other, they tucked into the paella, which the old lady declared to be the best she had ever tasted.

Warmed by her pleasure, Sophia put aside her low spirits and made a real effort to be cheerful. She succeeded so well that, after she had cleared away and stacked the dishwasher, they talked and laughed and played cribbage until almost eleven o'clock.

Suddenly catching sight of the time, she cried, 'Good gracious, I'd better get off home and let you go to bed.'

With Mrs Caldwell's thanks still ringing in her ears, she hurried back across the hall and unlocking her door, went inside and switched on the light.

The first thing she noticed were her keys lying just under the edge of the coffee table. She must have knocked them on to the floor when she'd moved the bag of shopping.

She had closed the door behind her and stooped to pick them up when a sudden strange, unprecedented feeling of unease made her stiffen and glance around.

Nothing seemed out of place and her handbag was where she'd left it, but a sixth sense insisted that something was wrong. Not as it had been.

But what?

Still puzzling, she dropped one set of keys into her handbag and put the spare ones back into the sideboard drawer, while she continued to look around.

Yes, that was it! At both the front window and the kitchen window at the side of the house, the curtains, which had been open, were now closed.

The fine hairs on the back of her neck rose and her skin goosefleshed as though a cool breeze had blown over it, while her thoughts flew backwards and forwards.

Someone must have been in the flat after she had gone across to Mrs Caldwell's.

Impossible. There was only the old lady and herself in the house.

However, the fact remained that curtains didn't draw themselves. And they must have been drawn for some specific *reason*.

It seemed to point to a burglar, or someone with nefarious intentions who hadn't wanted to be seen by anyone passing.

But the back door was always kept locked and bolted and no one could come in the front way who didn't ring one of the flats or have a key.

Yet someone had been in.

And perhaps still was.

Chilled by the thought, she shivered.

Then, nerving herself, she went to look, switching on lights as she went.

The bathroom door was ajar and it only took a moment to satisfy herself that no one was in there.

Then she opened the door of her father's studio and, her nostrils full of the familiar smell of paints and turpentine that lingered even now, looked around.

Apart from his easel, his unused canvases propped against a wall and, on the racks, his paints and brushes, his pallet and pallet knife, his cleaning fluids and soft rags, it was empty.

His bedroom too was free of intruders.

It was still as he had left it.

One of these days she would have to go through his private papers, and give his clothes and belongings to charity, but the grief was still too new, too raw, to be able to do it yet.

The only thing she had moved had been his last gift to her,

which she had discovered hidden in his bureau, along with some letters.

Though only about the size of a small shoebox, it had been quite heavy. Wrapped in gold paper, it bore a printed tag which had read simply:

For Sophia, with all my love. Have a very happy twenty-fifth birthday.

Finding it like that had made her tears flow.

When they were under control, she had stripped off the paper with unsteady fingers to reveal the exquisite ebony jewellery box that the stranger had commented on.

It was like a miniature chest, the thick, arched lid beautifully carved with what appeared to be one of the signs of the zodiac. A moment or two later, though it wasn't the conventional portrayal, she recognized it as Pisces, her own birth sign.

Caught in a curling wave were two tiny sea horses, one obviously frolicking, the other melancholy. It perfectly captured the dual personality, the moods and emotional depths, attributed to Pisceans.

Fresh tears had trickled down her cheeks while she wondered where her father—who had been housebound for quite some time—had managed to find such a lovely and appropriate birthday gift.

Her heart overflowing with love and gratitude, she had put it on her dressing table where she could see it the moment she woke up.

Suppose it had gone?

Almost more concerned about losing her gift than the possibility of finding an intruder, she took a deep breath and, flinging open her bedroom door, switched on the light.

To her immense relief the box was where she'd left it and

the room appeared to be empty, but—sensitive to atmosphere—
to Sophia it didn't *feel* empty.

Her divan bed was only an inch or two from the floor, so the
only place anyone could possibly hide was the walk-in wardrobe.

Though she told herself she was being a fool, she slid aside
the doors and peered in.

It occurred to her with wry amusement that if she *did* find
anyone hiding in there, she would probably die of fright.

In the event, it was innocent of anything but clothes and
accessories.

As she caught sight of the box once more, the thought struck
her that it was the right shape and size to be the package brought
by the mysterious visitor Mrs Caldwell had let in.

Maybe it had been a special delivery ordered by phone? If
that was the case, it would account for her father not mention-
ing anything about a visitor.

The fact that the man had been Italian was no doubt quite
irrelevant.

But would a delivery of that kind be made by taxi?

Well, the box had come from somewhere.

Giving up the riddle, her thoughts went back to a possible
burglar. The box was still here, but what about its contents?

Mostly it was costume stuff. The only items of any real value
were her few good pieces of jewellery and her father's signet
ring… But surely any would-be thief would have taken them?

A glance inside showed that nothing was missing, so maybe
the whole concept of a burglar had sprung from her imagination?

But what about the curtains?

Perhaps, her mind taken up with the fair-haired stranger, she
had closed them herself without registering the fact?

As if to add weight to this theory, she realized that none of
the curtains at the rear of the house had been closed.

Common sense jumped in and pointed out that they wouldn't

need to be. The garden was surrounded by a high wall, so no one could have looked in and noticed anything amiss.

Oh, well, *if* someone had come in—and it was starting to look less likely—they had gone out again without taking anything or doing any damage, so she must try and put the whole thing out of her mind.

She was about to move away and prepare for bed when she caught sight of something that looked like a wisp of stocking dangling from the drawer she kept her underwear in.

Frowning a little, she pulled it open to find that one of her fine silk stockings had somehow escaped from its protective wrapper and snagged on the top of the drawer.

She stared at it, a chill running through her, certain, or *almost* certain, that she hadn't left it like that.

A quick glance in her other drawers suggested that someone had looked through them, leaving them marginally less neat.

But, if that was so, as well as the puzzling—how did they get in? was the equally perplexing—what had they been looking for?

While she showered, brushed her teeth and put on her night-dress, she turned the whole thing over and over in her mind, but it made no sense.

By the time she climbed into bed, heartily sick of the fruitless exercise, she determined to think no more about it.

At once, thoughts of the fascinating stranger who had looked so like the man in her portrait brought to life flooded in.

The joy she'd felt on first seeing him came back to linger like some sad ghost. And she knew now that, as though under a spell, she had spent all her life just waiting for him.

But a one-sided enchantment was no use, and that was all it had been. Otherwise he wouldn't have walked away as casually as he had.

So what was the point of repining?

None at all, she told herself stoutly. She would try not to think about him. Though, with his face only a few feet away, that was easier said than done.

Reaching out a hand, she switched off the light, but blotting out sight did't stop the thoughts and regrets that tramped ceaselessly on the treadmill of her mind.

She slept badly, tossing and turning restlessly, and awoke headachy and unrefreshed to find the light of another grey, overcast day filling the room.

A bleary glance at her bedside clock showed that, for once in her life, she had badly overslept.

As quickly as possible, she showered and dressed in a neat business suit, coiled her dark hair and put on a hasty dab of make-up. Then, having swallowed a cup of instant coffee, she pulled on her coat and made her way to A Volonté.

Despite walking fast, she was over half an hour late by the time she hurried through the heavy smoked glass doors into the oval-shaped gallery.

Quiet and elegant, with its white, gold and dark green decor, its graceful sweep of staircase, its classic columns, which supported the encircling balcony, it was a Mecca for the art world.

On her way to the staff room, she glanced up at the balcony. Several people were already strolling round looking at her father's paintings. At the far end a couple with their backs to her—a tall fair-haired man and a petite woman with a black shoulder-length bob, were studying the miniatures.

The exhibition appeared to be getting off to a good start, thank the Lord.

When Sophia had hung up her coat and tapped on David's office door to give him her apologies—which he waved away— she went back to take her place at the discreetly positioned desk.

Over in the lounge area she could see Joanna sitting on one

of the dark green velvet couches talking to a balding man she recognized as a Parisian art critic and private collector.

A glance at the balcony showed the woman was still admiring the miniatures, while her companion had moved away a little and was looking at a collection of Venetian scenes which had been hung together.

More people were starting to drift in, but the gallery's policy was to let them browse in peace until they had a question to ask or were ready to buy, so Sophie turned her attention to the latest auction room catalogues.

There was a Joshua Roache coming up next week, and an early Cass that David might be interested in for his private collection…

A woman's voice said, '*Scusi signorina…*'

Putting the catalogue to one side, Sophia looked up with a smile. 'How can I help you?'

Judging by the smooth bell of black hair, it was the same woman who had been up on the balcony a few minutes ago.

She was extremely well dressed and vividly beautiful, with large black eyes, a creamy skin, a straight nose and full red lips. Her figure was voluptuous, her scarlet-tipped hands smooth and plump. As well as several dress rings, she wore a wide chased wedding band and a magnificent matching diamond solitaire.

At close quarters, Sophia could see she was somewhat older than she had first appeared, probably in her middle thirties.

In fluent but heavily accented English, she said, 'I would like to know more about this picture…'

To Sophia's dismay, she had taken down the miniature that Mrs Caldwell had remarked was both her favourite and Peter's.

Stretching out a hand, and trying hard to keep her voice even, Sophia suggested, 'Perhaps you'd like to give it to me?'

In spite of all her efforts, it must have sounded too much like an order because, with a haughty look, the woman informed her, 'You are talking to the Marquise d'Orsini.'

'I'm sorry, but no one is allowed to remove any of the paintings.'

'You do not understand. I intend to buy it.'

'I'm afraid it's not for sale.'

'How can you say such a thing?' the Marquise cried angrily. 'An art gallery exists to sell paintings, does it not?'

Aware that the woman's raised voice was attracting curious glances, Sophia said soothingly, 'Of course. All the paintings on this floor are for sale, including some excellent miniatures.'

'But it is *this* one I want.'

'I'm extremely sorry, but that one and the other miniatures on the balcony are part of a Peter Jordan exhibition, and not for sale.'

'Nonsense! I wish you to—'

Sophia heard no more as, glancing up, she saw a tall, good-looking man approaching. He was dressed in smart casuals, his carriage was easy and there was a quiet assurance in the way he held his blond head. His dark grey eyes were fixed on her face.

Rooted to the spot, she gazed at the man she had never seriously expected to see again.

Was his coming into A Volonté a coincidence?

No, surely not.

A surge of gladness filled her and brought a glorious smile to her face.

He smiled back, that white, slightly crooked smile that made her feel hollow inside.

The Marquise, realizing she had lost Sophia's attention, turned and, seeing him, grasped his arm and broke into a rapid stream of Italian. 'This girl had the nerve to tell me I shouldn't have taken down the miniature—'

Speaking in the same language, he said, 'Didn't I advise you not to?'

Her hot temper making her reckless, she snapped, 'I get tired of being "advised" what to do. Men always think they are right. They always say, "I told you so". You should be on my side, not agreeing with this insolent chit of a girl who—'

Putting a finger to her carmine lips to interrupt the flow, he warned, 'It's quite likely that the *signorina* speaks Italian… She is—'

'I know what she is… A little nobody with an inflated sense of her own importance. Well, she's making a mistake if she thinks she can—'

'*Cara*, you are the one who is making the mistake. I advise you to calm down and—'

'I don't need advice,' she flared. 'I will act as I think fit.'

'Very well.'

Though he spoke quietly, without any trace of anger, she clutched at his arm. 'Stefano, darling, I'm sorry, so sorry. I shouldn't have snapped at you like that…'

When he said nothing, tears welling in her black eyes, she whispered, 'Forgive me. I had no right to get angry with *you*…'

Watching his face soften, Sophia wondered—was he this beautiful woman's husband?

The thought made her feel as though she'd been punched in the solar plexus.

Even if he wasn't, he was almost certainly her *amante*. There was no other way to explain the feeling of intimacy between them, the possessive touch of her hand on his sleeve, the way she was gazing up at him. Her voice soft, seductive, she begged, 'Please tell me what I should do.'

'I suggest you apologize to the *signorina* and return the painting.'

'Apologize! But Stefano—'

'It might be expedient,' he told her.

After a moment or two of silence, she turned to Sophia and, handing her the miniature, said grudgingly in English, 'I am sorry.'

'That's quite all right,' Sophia assured her pleasantly, and even managed a smile.

Looking far from mollified, the Marquise said, 'I understand that the artist is no longer living?'

'No, unfortunately he died early in March.'

'Perhaps *you* can tell me who the sitter was and precisely when it was painted?'

'I'm afraid I can't.'

Glaring at Sophia, as if she were being deliberately obstructive, the Marquise ordered, 'Then give me a catalogue, so I can look for myself.'

Handing her a catalogue, Sophia told her politely, 'The miniature is listed on page twelve. You'll find it just says, *Portrait of a Venetian Lady at Carnival Time*.'

Throwing the catalogue angrily on to the desk, the Marquise said, 'I have wasted enough time. I want to buy this picture and I—'

'I'm sorry but, as I've already explained, it isn't for sale.'

'I have had more than enough of your impertinence…'

The man she had called Stefano put a warning hand on her arm but, too furious to heed it, she rushed on, 'I insist on speaking to the owner of the gallery or someone in authority.'

'Very well.' Sophia picked up the phone and, when David's voice answered, asked quietly, 'Could you please come to the desk?'

Alerted by her tone, he asked, 'Trouble?'

'Yes, I'm afraid so.' Replacing the receiver, she braced herself for the storm she could see was about to burst.

'You may well look apprehensive,' the Marquise cried. 'If

you think you can treat me like this and get away with it, you are mistaken. I will make sure you lose your job and—'

'That's enough, Gina.' The man by her side spoke with a quiet authority that brought the Marquise up short. 'You're making a spectacle of yourself.'

After that first smile, Sophia had never looked directly at him, but she had been conscious of his presence. And, while the surface of her mind had been taken up with the Marquise, her whole being had been focused on him, aware of his steady regard, aware too of the unspoken empathy.

At that instant David appeared, immaculately dressed, a cream carnation in his buttonhole, and approached the little group.

Of medium height, he was a slim, elegant bachelor in his early fifties, an art connoisseur to his fingertips. His silvery hair worn slightly long, his pale blue eyes guileless, his air of *bonhomie*, all combined to disguise the fact that he was also a shrewd, hard-headed businessman.

'Is there a problem?' he asked mildly.

'Indeed there is. I am the Marquise d'Orsini, and this chit of a girl—'

He gave her a courteous little bow, stopping the threatening torrent of words. 'And I'm David Renton, owner of A Volonté. If you and the Marquis would—'

'I'm afraid you're under a misapprehension,' the other man broke in with grave politeness. 'I'm not the Marquis. My name's Stephen Haviland.'

So he wasn't the Marquise's husband after all. Sophia experienced such a rush of relief she felt almost giddy.

As the two men shook hands, his glance and his smile including the Marquise in his apology, David murmured smoothly, 'I *do* beg your pardon.'

Obviously won over by his charm, she said, 'Please do not apologize, Mr Renton. It was an easy mistake to make.'

'You're very forgiving. Now, if you and Mr Haviland would care to come through to my private suite, I'm sure we can sort things out to your satisfaction.'

As the Marquise flashed Sophia a look of malicious triumph, David continued avuncularly, 'Will you please come too, Sophia, my dear?'

Sophia was aware that David had intended the 'my dear' to be both a statement and a subtle warning to the Marquise of where he himself stood.

Lifting a hand, he signalled to Joanna that the desk was un-attended. Then, his smile pleasant, his manner affable, he turned to usher them through to his inner sanctum.

As Sophia made to follow, Stephen Haviland stood to one side to allow her to precede him.

With a murmur of thanks, she did so.

David's sitting-room was quietly luxurious, with beautiful antique furniture, an Oriental carpet, two soft natural leather couches, a designer blind at the window and a small semicir-cular bar in one corner. Pictures, each worth a small fortune, lined the walls and fresh flowers scented the air.

Waving a well-manicured hand, David said, 'Won't you sit down?'

The Marquise settled herself on the nearest couch and, with an inviting glance at Stephen Haviland, patted the seat beside her.

'Sophia, my dear, perhaps you'll sit here?' David sug-gested blandly.

Stephen Haviland remained standing until Sophia was seated on the other couch.

David produced a bottle of fine old sherry and four spark-ling crystal glasses and, at his most urbane, asked, 'May I offer you a glass of sherry?'

'That would be very nice,' the Marquise accepted graciously.

The sherry poured and handed out, David took a seat by Sophia's side. 'Now, how can I help?'

The Marquise had obviously read into David's attitude towards Sophia what he had intended her to read and, instead of launching into a denunciation, she began carefully, 'I am afraid your employee and I…how do you say…got off on the wrong feet. I made an error of judgement, for which I have already made my apologies…'

When he merely waited politely, she went on, 'I took down one of the pictures, a miniature. I hoped to buy it, but I was told it was not for sale.'

'May I ask which one?'

'The catalogue described it as a *Portrait of a Venetian Lady at Carnival Time*.'

'I'm afraid that particular miniature forms part of our current exhibition and is merely on loan.' As though to make it quite plain, he added, 'It doesn't belong to the gallery.'

'Perhaps you can tell me who it *does* belong to?'

In response to David's glance, Sophia said quietly, 'It belongs to me.'

'It belongs to you?' the Marquise repeated after a moment as though doubting her ears.

'Yes.'

'Then why did you refuse to tell me who the sitter was and when it was painted?' she demanded angrily.

'I'm sorry, but I don't *know*. My father painted the portrait many years ago, before I was born.'

'Your father… Then you must be…'

'Sophia Jordan,' Sophia agreed.

The Marquise turned to Stephen and, in Italian, began, 'Why didn't you—?' Seeing the unmistakable glint in his eye, she broke off abruptly.

For a moment or two there was silence, then, rallying, the

Marquise addressed Sophia and, speaking English now, said earnestly, 'Signorina Jordan, I would very much like to add the miniature to my collection. I am willing to pay well.'

'I'm sorry to disappoint you but, as I said earlier, it isn't for sale.'

The Marquise bit her lip. 'I know we have got off on the wrong feet, but—'

'Believe me, it has nothing to do with that. My father's paintings are precious to me and I have no intention of parting with any of them.'

Seeing how downcast she looked, Sophia felt almost sorry for this fiery-natured woman.

'Perhaps you would care to see the miniatures that are for sale?' David suggested. 'There are some extremely fine ones, and two that are very like the portrait of a Venetian lady.'

'Thank you, but no.'

'Then is there anything else I can do for you?'

As she started to shake her head, Stephen Haviland said, 'We're flying back to Venice today…'

We're flying back to Venice today… Did that mean he was *living* in Venice? Sophia wondered.

'Which means we have to start for the airport shortly, but I would be grateful if you could spare just a few more minutes.'

'Of course,' David agreed politely. 'In what way can I help?'

'There's a somewhat urgent matter I would like to discuss with you…'

Sophia rose. 'If you'll excuse me, I should get back to the desk.'

'Please don't go, Miss Jordan,' Stephen Haviland said. His grey eyes on her face, he added, 'As what I'm about to ask particularly concerns you, your presence is essential.'

She resumed her seat, satisfied that this was merely a further attempt—on his part—to persuade her to sell the miniature.

Judging by the hopeful glance the Marquise gave him, she thought so too.

He put down his sherry glass and, his eyes on Sophia's face and his long, well-shaped hands resting lightly on his knees, began, 'I'll endeavour to be as brief as possible while I put you in the picture.

'When my aunt died earlier this year, she left me the Fortuna family home in Venice…'

He paused, almost as if he were expecting some reaction from her.

When she just waited quietly, he went on, 'The Palazzo del Fortuna is a beautiful place but, with the decline of the family fortunes over the last couple of hundred years, unfortunately it has been somewhat neglected.

'When my aunt discovered that one wing of the Palazzo was sinking and in urgent need of substantial structural repairs, she asked me for financial help, which I was more than willing to provide.

'As soon as the money was made available she brought in the builders, but as the work progressed it became clear that it was going to cost a great deal more than originally estimated…'

'Isn't that always the way?' David murmured.

'Too true,' Stephen Haviland agreed. He added, 'Luckily it wasn't a problem, and the restoration was finished on time.

'But, in order to have some spare money in hand for the ordinary day-to-day maintenance, and unwilling to accept any more help from me, my aunt made up her mind to sell some of the paintings which have been in the family for many generations.

'Museums and art galleries worldwide and a number of rich private collectors expressed their interest, and she engaged an expert from Milan to examine the paintings in order to assess their value and condition, and also to do any cleaning and restoring that might prove to be necessary.

'That done, she went on to plan a series of private viewings for the interested parties, but no sooner were all the arrangements in place than she became ill and died within quite a short space of time.

'It was her stated wish that when I took over I should carry through the plans she had made. The first viewing is scheduled to take place in just over six weeks' time…'

It was all very interesting, Sophia thought, but what had it to do with her?

With his next words, Stephen Haviland answered that unspoken question.

'The expert my aunt engaged was due at the Palazzo on Monday to start getting the first batch of paintings ready. But just this morning I heard that he had been injured in a road accident and would be unable to fulfil his commitments. So I'm in urgent need of someone to step into his shoes.'

Turning to Sophia, he went on levelly, 'When we were talking last night you mentioned that, as well as assessing their value, part of your job was cleaning and restoring old paintings…'

Though David never so much as batted an eyelid, Sophia could tell he was surprised to learn that they had met before.

'If Mr Renton can spare you for a few weeks and you're willing to come to Venice,' Stephen Haviland went on, 'you're just the woman I need.'

The thought of keeping contact, of actually going to Venice to work for him, made excitement run through her veins like molten lava.

Catching sight of the dismay on the older woman's face was like a douche of cold water.

'What are you thinking of, Stefano?' the Marquise said sharply. 'Surely you could find someone closer to home?'

'No doubt. But it would take time, and time is something I don't have.'

Turning back to Sophia, he added, 'I would be prepared to pay whatever salary you ask, and meet all your travelling expenses. You would, of course, stay at Ca' Fortuna.

'Have you ever been to Venice?'

She shook her head. 'Though my mother was born at Mestre, I've never visited the area at all.'

'In that case, this would be an excellent opportunity to combine business with pleasure.'

Then, addressing David, 'As far as you're concerned, Mr Renton, I'm willing to compensate you for losing Miss Jordan's services by giving you first choice of the paintings at ten per cent less than their agreed market value.'

'That's very generous,' David said slowly, 'and for my part I have no objection to the plan, but of course it's up to Sophia.'

'Perhaps you would like a few minutes of privacy to discuss it?' Stephen suggested.

'An excellent idea,' David said briskly. 'If you and the Marquise would be kind enough to wait here? May I offer you more sherry?'

Having refilled their glasses, he led Sophia through to his office.

As they left the room she heard the Marquise—who since her previous outburst had been sitting still and silent—break into a flood of Italian.

'You must be stark staring mad to consider bringing *her* to the Palazzo. What good can it possibly do? And it will be playing clean into the girl's hands if she has any…'

The door closing behind them cut off the rest.

CHAPTER THREE

DAVID'S office, with its large imposing desk and state-of-the-art technology, was as businesslike as his sitting-room was sumptuous.

Waving Sophia to a black leather chair, he said, 'Sit down, my dear.'

She obeyed, the hostile words she had just overheard still echoing in her ears. *You must be stark raving mad to consider bringing her to the Palazzo...*

The Marquise had said *bringing* rather than *taking,* which strongly suggested that the Palazzo del Fortuna was *her* home too. And what had she meant by, *it will be playing clean into the girl's hands?*

Watching Sophia's abstracted face, David perched on the edge of his desk. After a moment or two, he said, 'Far be it for me to pry, but how long have you known Mr Haviland?'

She blinked before answering, 'We met last night.' Leaving out any of the deeper aspects, she briefly explained the circumstances. 'He told me he was flying home today, so I really hadn't expected to see him again.'

David could sense her reaction from the tone of her voice. 'But you were pleased to?'

'Yes.' Sophia nodded shyly.

'And the Marquise?'

'Today is the first time we've met.'

'I won't ask you if you liked her,' David said dryly. 'Reading between the lines, I imagine she made herself quite unpleasant.'

'I'm afraid so,' Sophia agreed.

'So how do you feel about going to Venice?'

'It's something I've always dreamt of. Dad, who knew the city well, always said that one day we'd go. But somehow we never got there…'

'Does that mean you're considering accepting Haviland's proposition?'

'I'd very much like to… But I'm not sure.'

'Because of the Marquise?'

'Well, yes.'

'Perhaps you wouldn't need to come into contact with her,' David said practically.

Sophia shook her head. 'From the way she spoke about the Palazzo, I get the distinct impression that that's where she lives.'

'Even if she does, if you feel like taking the job, don't let her put you off.' David smiled, keen that Sophia make the choice that she wanted, without the influence of the Marquise.

'She doesn't want me there.'

'Judging by what he's prepared to offer, Haviland certainly does,' David countered her argument. 'And, if you don't want to risk living under the same roof as the Marquise, you can always insist on staying at a hotel.'

When she said nothing, he asked shrewdly, 'Something else bothering you?'

'She's very beautiful.' Sophia made an effort not to sound wistful.

'And married.'

'Yes, I know, but…'

'You still think that she and Haviland are rather more than just good friends?'

'Don't you?' she countered.

'It's possible,' David replied cautiously. 'But, though they obviously know one another very well, from what I've seen of his attitude towards her, I tend to think not…'

David was a good judge of human nature, and his answer—combined with the thought that if Stephen and the Marquise were lovers, he would hardly have asked *her* out—made Sophia's spirits rise.

'In any case it's really none of my business,' David went on. 'And it's certainly not like you to worry about other people's morals.'

Then, his glance sharpening, 'Unless… Do I take it you're seriously interested in him?'

'Yes,' she admitted.

'If you don't accept his offer, what are the chances of seeing him again?'

'Nil, I imagine.'

'You've been looking peaky lately. I think a complete break and some Italian sunshine is just what you need. You may come back feeling a new woman.'

'And I may come back with a broken heart.' She spoke the thought aloud.

David had known Sophia since she was a girl and was well aware that where men were concerned she tended to remain cool, unmoved, a veritable ice queen. Even after her engagement had ended, she had never spoken the words *a broken heart*.

Now, hiding his surprise that she should use them about a man she had only just met, he said firmly, 'Then again, you may not.'

'She's a very beautiful woman,' Sophia repeated.

'So are you.'

Sophia, who had no great appreciation of her own looks, half shook her head.

'Plus *you* have a lovely nature,' David went on, 'and in the long run it's what's underneath that really counts.'

Seriously, he added, 'I'd like you to be happy, my dear, so if you feel Haviland may be the man for you, go and give this thing a chance.

'Of course on closer acquaintance he may turn out to be so obnoxious you wouldn't have him as a gift. But until you're sure, then my advice is to ignore the Marquise and stay at the Palazzo, fight for him if you have to.'

Thinking of the other woman's vivid beauty and voluptuous figure, Sophia said wryly, 'I'm afraid I can't see myself winning, and I don't want to forfeit my self-respect.'

'Knowing you, I've no fear of that. And if you don't try, if you chicken out and stay at home, you'll have lost anyway.'

'You're right, of course. But there's a snag…'

'What's that?'

She made a self-deprecating moue. 'I don't know how to… Fight for a man, I mean.'

David laughed, as she had intended him to do. 'Just be yourself. Now, shall we go back and give Haviland the good news? Oh, by the way, if you have any stipulations, don't hesitate to say so.'

When they returned to the other room, the Marquise and Stephen Haviland, her gleaming black head and his blond one close together, were deep in a low-toned, earnest conversation.

If they weren't lovers they were certainly very old and intimate friends, Sophia thought as, breaking off, Stephen rose to his feet and, his eyes on her face, asked evenly, 'So what's the verdict?'

Only too aware that the Marquise was going to be anything but pleased by her acceptance of the proposition, Sophia began, 'I would be happy to come to Venice…'

He smiled at her and took her breath away.

Hearing David clear his throat, she added hastily, 'On one condition.'

'Name it.'

'I would prefer to stay at a hotel rather than at the Palazzo del Fortuna.' She hoped very much that he wouldn't ask why.

He didn't. 'Certainly, if that's what you want,' he agreed. Then, crisply, 'Can you be ready to travel by Monday afternoon?'

'Yes,' she answered without hesitation, 'so long as I can get a flight.'

'Though the Venetian tourist season is well under way, as you'll be travelling mid-week there shouldn't be too much of a problem. Now, would you like me to make the arrangements, or would you prefer to make them yourself?'

After a moment's consideration, deciding she would prefer to have a free hand, she said, 'I'll make them, thank you.'

'Have you any particular hotel in mind?'

She shook her head.

'Then may I suggest you try the Tre Pozzi? Without being luxurious, it's both comfortable and central...I presume you can speak Italian?'

'Yes. My mother always spoke to me in Italian and for some years after her death my father carried on the practice.'

The Marquise looked momentarily discomposed, while Stephen Haviland nodded his approval, before saying, 'I'll give you the phone number.' He produced a pen from his jacket pocket and, on a page torn from a small diary, jotted it down.

'And this is my home number... When all the arrangements are in place and you know the time of your arrival, perhaps you'll give me a ring?'

'Of course.'

He held out his hand and, with a strange feeling of having irrevocably committed herself, she put hers into it.

It was the first time he had touched her and, as his strong

fingers closed around her slender ones, every nerve in her body responded to that touch and her heart lurched crazily.

Even when his grip loosened, it was a moment or two before she was able to withdraw her hand.

Turning to David, he said, 'Thank you for your time and for loaning me Miss Jordan. If you would like to come to Venice yourself and take a look at the paintings, you're welcome to stay at Ca' Fortuna.'

David murmured his thanks and the two men shook hands cordially.

The Marquise rose to her feet and held out her hand with a forced smile, 'Thank you, and goodbye.'

Taking her proffered hand, David bowed over it. 'May I wish you a pleasant journey home.'

Turning to Sophia, the Marquise said stiffly, 'I'll see you in Venice, Signorina Jordan.'

As David opened the door to escort them back to the gallery, his phone started to ring. Excusing himself, he went back to answer it, leaving Sophia to show them out.

When they reached the main entrance, the Marquise said in an urgent undertone, 'If you should change your mind about the miniature, I will give you whatever you ask.'

'I'm sorry, but I won't change my mind.'

As, muttering something under her breath, the other woman turned away abruptly and stepped out on to the pavement, Stephen Haviland apologized quietly. 'I hope you'll forgive such persistence.'

'I don't understand what makes that miniature so special,' Sophia remarked helplessly. 'As David said, there are others for sale that are equally fine, if not better.'

'Gina has set her heart on that particular one,' he answered smoothly, 'and she can't bear to be disappointed. She has always been a creature of strong passions…'

She has always been a creature of strong passions... It sounded as if he had known the Marquise for a very long time.

'Anything she wants,' Stephen Haviland went on, 'she wants fiercely, much the same as a child. But please don't let it bother you...'

Smiling down at Sophia, he added, 'Now I'll say *arrivederci* until Monday.'

'Until Monday,' she echoed, her heart filling with hope and happiness.

Though his words had been mundane, superficial, the look in his grey eyes had made them into something special, deeper. A promise. A tryst. A dream that might well come true.

Her travel arrangements made, as promised, Sophia phoned Stephen Haviland. Just the sound of his cool, attractive voice—so clear and close he could have been standing by her side—made her heart beat faster and sent a quiver running through her.

Gathering herself, she said, 'Mr Haviland, it's Sophia Jordan...'

'As we'll be working together for some weeks, won't you make it Stephen? And may I call you Sophia?'

'Of course.'

'So is everything fixed, Sophia?'

'Yes, I've managed to book a seat on a plane leaving at two-forty. The flight number is...'

While she filled in the details he listened without interruption, then said, 'I'll make sure there's someone at the airport to meet you...

'By the way, we're having a heatwave in Venice, so bring something cool and summery... Oh, and a swimsuit... You can swim?'

She said, 'Yes, but not very well, I'm afraid. I haven't been swimming since my school days.'

'Then I'll take you over to the Lido and you can get some practice in.'

His voice growing warmer, more intimate, he added softly, 'I'm looking forward to seeing you again. *Arrivederci*, Sophia.'

'*Arrivederci*…'

'Stephen,' he prompted.

'Stephen,' she echoed, while a little thrill of excitement made butterflies dance in her stomach.

A small but versatile wardrobe was laid out on her bed ready to pack and, unwilling to be parted from it, her jewellery box.

Now, her stomach still feeling fluttery, she added several more lightweight dresses and another pair of sandals before putting everything neatly in her case.

When she had unearthed her swimsuit she found it was distinctly schoolgirlish and far too tight across the bust. With a grimace she thrust it back in the drawer, deciding that if she needed a swimsuit she would buy one.

Her packing finished, she went across the hall to see Mrs Caldwell. Eva was still at church, so they had a cup of coffee together while Sophia told her the news.

After thinking about it, Sophia had decided to say only that she was going to Venice on a working holiday, but even that was enough to start the old lady off.

'How exciting! Italian men are the most romantic in the world… I used to fancy Rossano Brazzi, myself. He was gorgeous! Such a fascinating accent! And then there was… I can see his face but I just forget his name… Though they would be before your time…'

Mrs Caldwell was still in full flow when Eva returned and Sophia was able to make her escape.

'I'll say goodbye now in case I don't see you before I go.'

'Well just make the most of it, my dear, and don't work too hard.'

'If it's all right with you, as I'm leaving I'll put my key through your door so you can keep an eye on the flat.'

'Of course it's all right. Now don't forget to send Eva and me a card.'

'I won't.'

Monday proved to be another overcast and somewhat chilly day and a light rain was falling when she boarded her plane early that afternoon.

The flight was routine and uneventful, but to Sophia it was the most exciting and enjoyable trip she had ever taken.

Just the thought of being in Venice, the city of her dreams, with the man of her dreams, a man who had said—as if he really meant it—'I'm looking forward to seeing you again', made her feel on top of the world.

But she mustn't attach too much importance to what might have been uttered out of sheer politeness, and she mustn't let her hopes rise too high.

Leaving aside any possible involvement with the Marquise, Stephen Haviland was obviously a wealthy man from a privileged background, while *she* was just an ordinary working girl.

But no amount of lecturing herself was able to quell an excitement which rose to fever pitch when the flight captain announced that they were approaching Marco Polo Airport and would be landing shortly.

They descended from a cloudless blue sky into a shimmering heat that gave planes and airport buildings alike the unreal quality of a mirage, and when, along with a stream of passengers, Sophia left the aircraft, it was like walking into an oven.

She could feel the tarmac burning through the thin soles of her court shoes and the lightweight suit she had chosen to travel in now seemed too warm.

Italy, with its heat and blazing sunshine, seemed a world away from the cool greyness she had left behind in England.

Her luggage collected and the formalities over, unable to find a baggage trolley, she was struggling to make her way across the crowded terminal when a voice she was starting to know well, said, 'Ciao,' and Stephen Haviland materialized at her elbow.

Casually dressed in light trousers and a silk, short-sleeved shirt he looked tanned and fit and extremely handsome.

Struck dumb, she was still gaping at him when he remarked, a shade mockingly, 'You look surprised to see me.'

Finding her voice, she blurted out, 'You didn't say *you* would be meeting me.'

'I wasn't certain I could get away.'

He took her case and, a hand at her waist, shepherded her towards the exit, bending towards her to query politely, 'I hope you had a good flight.'

She could smell the faint masculine scent of his aftershave and, her wits scattered by his nearness, she stammered, 'Y-yes, very good, thank you.'

Once outside, he led the way to a sleek white open-topped car and, having put her luggage in the boot, helped her into the front passenger seat before sliding behind the wheel.

As he reached over to fasten her seat belt, his hand brushed her thigh.

Just that lightest of accidental touches made every nerve in her body tingle and sent a wave of heat running through her.

Knowing she was blushing, she told herself crossly that it was time she stopped reacting like an overgrown schoolgirl and started to behave with her usual cool composure.

His grey eyes studying her face, he remarked, 'You look a little warm.'

Taking a deep breath, she said, 'I am,' and was pleased to find her voice sounded almost normal.

'Let me…' He helped her off with her jacket.

'Thank you, that's much better. Though you mentioned it was hot in Venice, I hadn't expected anything like this.'

'Do you dislike the heat, Sophia?'

'Oh, no, I love it.'

As the engine purred into life, he remarked, 'Perhaps that's just as well, because it looks set to continue for a while.'

Once they were on their way, the flow of air cooled her flushed cheeks and, to some extent, restored her equilibrium.

He drove with care and skill through the busy airport traffic, then with a laid-back ease that made the journey a pleasure.

His hands, she noticed, were lean and tanned with long fingers and neatly trimmed nails, his wrists strong, the left one wearing a thin platinum watch. His arms were muscular, with a fine sprinkling of golden hair that gleamed in the sun.

She was wondering what it would feel like to have those arms around her, when he turned his head to glance at her.

For just a heartbeat grey eyes met and held green.

Feeling her cheeks grow hot once more, she looked hastily away.

'We're approaching Mestre now,' he told her after another mile or so, 'and Venice itself is just across the causeway.'

Staring out at the flat, unprepossessing countryside with its widespread industrialization, Sophia found it almost impossible to believe that the shining dream of Venice lay so close at hand.

As though reading her thoughts, Stephen remarked, 'Your first sight of Venice should really have been from the lagoon. That way its beauty can be properly appreciated. But I'm afraid I had some business that necessitated bringing the car.'

'I thought there were no cars in Venice.'

'There aren't. The Piazzale Roma, on the far side of the causeway, is as far as we can go. There the car is garaged and we go on by boat.

'We'll be reaching the causeway, or to give it its proper name, the Ponte della Liberta, in just a minute or so.'

Sophia was keen to see the picturesque Venice she had imagined. 'How long is it?'

'It's about three and a half kilometres in length and quite wide. As well as the road, it carries the railway… Ah, here we are.'

As they joined the busy causeway, with its lanes of vehicles and a series of railway tracks running to the left, Sophia looked in vain for the romantic Venice of her dreams.

'Don't be disappointed,' Stephen said, interpreting her silence correctly. 'This is the down-to-earth side of Venice.'

'You know the city well, presumably?'

'Very well. I was born at the Palazzo del Fortuna and spent the first seven years of my life there.

'I've always loved Venice and would have happily stayed here, but when my grandfather died and left my father his business empire, my parents decided to make their home in the USA…'

Eager to learn more about him, Sophia was about to ask some further questions when, as they reached the end of the causeway, he remarked, 'On your right are the main car parking facilities for tourists, and this is the Piazzale Roma.'

He stopped the car in front of what appeared to be a block of private garages and, when she had gathered up her shoulder bag and jacket, helped her out.

As he took her luggage from the boot, a uniformed attendant appeared and gave them a respectful salute.

Passing him the keys and some folded notes, Stephen said, 'Take care of it, will you, Luigi?'

'Certainly, Signor Haviland.'

A hand at Sophia's waist, Stephen shepherded her across the Piazzale, which was hot and dusty, noisy with buses and thronging with pedestrians.

On the far side were open stalls, some selling pizza and sandwiches and cold drinks, others displaying rosy black-seeded watermelon and thin white slices of coconut set out beneath sparkling jets of water.

They went down a short flight of steps on to a wide stone *fondamenta,* where Stephen paused and waited.

There, spread before her eyes with a suddenness that took her breath away, was the Grand Canal and the Venice of her dreams.

The canal was much wider than she had imagined. On its sparkling blue water were craft of all shapes and sizes—from the graceful black steel-prowed gondolas, through a range of motorboats, to a large *vaporetto* crowded with people.

Along the *fonda*, where wooden landing stages gave access to the waterbuses, a colourful jostle of stalls offered food, drinks, fruit, ice cream, dolls, glassware and tourist bric-à-brac.

Everywhere there was an air of *joie de vivre* and gaiety. Venice at its best, and Sophia was enchanted. When she finally lifted a glowing face to the man by her side, she found his eyes were fixed on her.

He nodded, as though understanding her feelings, and without a word to break the spell led her to the canal and down some old stone steps to where a small motorboat was moored.

Leaning over, he stowed her luggage, then steadied the craft with one sandalled foot while he handed her into it.

As soon as she was seated, he jumped down lightly and, casting off, took his place behind the wheel and started the engine.

As, keeping well into the right, they set off down the canal, he pointed across to the opposite bank where a large, relatively modern building stood back from a deep-paved frontage. 'That's Santa Lucia station. Quite a lot of visitors come by rail.'

A few moments later they went under a wide stone bridge, the only one in sight, and, almost to herself, Sophia remarked, 'I always imagined there would be lots of bridges.'

'There are. Hundreds. But only three, including the Rialto, cross the Grand Canal.'

Though, as he expertly manoeuvred the boat along the busy canal, he named some of the more important buildings they passed, he was mostly silent, giving her a chance to drink it all in.

Looking at the array of wonderful old buildings that lined its banks, the ornate marble palaces and magnificent churches, Sophia thought how odd it was that, though both her parents had known all this well, it was the first time she herself had seen it.

Yet, despite everything being strange and exotic, she felt at home here, as if she belonged.

Blinking a little in the brightness like a sleepy cat, the sun warm on her skin, a light breeze flicking an escaped tendril of dark hair against her cheek, she sighed contentedly.

As they passed a row of gay red and white striped poles lording it over the more sober black mooring posts, she roused herself to ask, 'How far is it to the Tre Pozzi?'

'Not far, but I was rather hoping you might have changed your mind about staying at a hotel.'

Taking a deep breath, she said evenly, 'As I have a room booked, it's a bit late to change my mind.'

'We could always cancel the booking. Venice is packed at the moment, and my guess is there are still plenty of tourists looking for accommodation, so the room will soon be snapped up.'

Giving her a smile that made her heart beat faster, he added, 'It would please me very much if you did decide to stay at Ca' Fortuna.'

Just for a moment Sophia was sorely tempted. Then, remembering the Marquise, she said, 'Thank you, but I think I'll stick with my original plan.'

'Very well,' he gave in gracefully. 'The Tre Pozzi it is.'

In a little while they left the Grand Canal and, after negotiating a maze of smaller waterways, drew into the landing stage of an ochre-coloured building four storeys high.

Peeling stucco and tall shuttered windows that opened on to narrow wrought iron balconies in need of a lick of paint, gave it an air of general seediness. Above the entrance was a fancy wooden scroll that read, 'Tre Pozzi'.

Stephen cut the engine and moored the boat, then, jumping out, he offered Sophia his hand, saying cheerfully, 'When you've booked in, someone will fetch your luggage.'

Catching sight of her expression, he laughed, white teeth gleaming, deep creases appearing each side of his mouth. 'Yes, it's what you might describe as picturesque decay. But don't worry; inside it's pleasant enough.'

Once through the heavy wooden doors she found that the lobby was attractive and well-furnished, with plants and ferns, cool terrazzo floors, sparkling chandeliers and long wall mirrors

At the reception desk she gave her name to a short balding man who opened the register and ran a finger rapidly down the page before shaking his head. 'I'm afraid we don't have a booking for a Signorina Jordan.'

'I phoned and reserved a room,' Sophia said firmly but pleasantly, 'so perhaps you would be good enough to check again?'

'A single room?' he queried.

'I was told there wouldn't be a single room available for a day or two, so I agreed to take a double *en suite* overlooking the campo.'

'And it was booked in the name of Jordan?'

'Yes.'

Without re-opening the register, the desk clerk made a dismissive gesture. 'I'm sorry, but we have no reservation in that name.'

Stephen, who had been standing to one side listening, said, 'Please do as the *signorina* asked, and check again.'

Though he spoke quietly there was an unmistakable note of authority in his voice that made the receptionist open and consult the register again without further delay.

After a moment or two he spread his hands, palms uppermost, and, his manner ingratiating now, reiterated, 'I very much regret, but we have no reservation for a Signorina Jordan.'

'Then perhaps you have a room of some kind?'

'I'm afraid not. Every room we have is occupied. When exactly did you phone, Signorina Jordan?'

'Yesterday morning.'

Spreading his hands once more, he admitted, 'Evidently there's been some mistake. All our rooms have been fully booked for the last two days.'

'Would it be possible to speak to the person I dealt with then?'

'The desk clerk who was on duty yesterday is off sick, so I'm afraid that at the moment I can offer no explanation as to how the mix-up came about. And unfortunately,' he added unctuously, 'it will be Thursday before we have a vacancy.'

Knowing it was useless to persist any further, and feeling guilty that she had already wasted so much of Stephen's time, Sophia said, 'Then perhaps you could suggest somewhere else I could try?'

He shook his head. 'Our sister hotel is fully booked, and I'm afraid you'll find that most of the hotels in the centre are full.'

Stifling a sigh, she thanked him and turned away.

As she did so, she caught sight of herself reflected in one of the long gilt-framed mirrors opposite—tall and slim in a silver-grey skirt and an ivory blouse, a jacket over her arm, a bag on her shoulder, one or two tendrils of dark curly hair escaping from her chignon.

Behind her, she saw Stephen give the desk clerk a little nod and they exchanged glances that made them look like conspirators, just as a little group of holiday-makers—lobster-red from the sun and hung with cameras—came crowding round the desk to pick up their keys.

A second later Stephen was by her side, escorting her out, his expression and his manner so normal she knew she must have misread that exchange of glances.

Handing her back into the boat, he waited until she was seated before stepping in and sitting down beside her. He was much too close for comfort and she had to resist the urge to inch away.

'As you're so set against staying at Ca' Fortuna,' he said a shade caustically, 'I've two suggestions to make. We could go to the Venice Tourist Bureau, who may be able to find you a room, or I could take you over to Ca' d'Orsini.'

'Ca' d'Orsini?' she echoed uncertainly.

'Gina's home. I'm sure she would be happy to accommodate you.'

Like hell she would! Sophia thought and, an instant later, dazzled by the realization, blurted out, 'Then the Marquise doesn't live at the Palazzo?'

Knowing the relief she felt must have been only too evident in her voice, she felt herself blushing.

His amused glance taking in her heightening colour, Stephen asked, 'What made you think she did?'

Reluctant to admit what she'd overheard, Sophia began weakly, 'She…she seemed to…'

'Regard it as her home?' he suggested, when she left the sentence hanging in mid air.

'Well, yes…'

'I suppose in a way that's understandable. You see, the Palazzo del Fortuna *was* Gina's home before she married the Marquis d'Orsini.'

'Oh…'

Sophia longed to know more but, as she hesitated, wondering how to frame her next question, Stephen went on crisply, 'So now we've got that sorted out, shall we head for the Palazzo?'

His voice sardonic, he added, 'Or do you still have reservations about staying there?'

Knowing she'd asked for it, but wanting to justify her stand, Sophia apologized. 'I'm sorry, but I…'

'Overheard what Gina said?' Stephen finished for her.

'Yes,' she admitted unwillingly.

Frowning, he asked, 'How much did you overhear?'

'Not a great deal.'

'Perhaps you'd like to tell me exactly?'

Feeling uncomfortable, she told him, ending, 'Then, just as the door was closing, I heard her say, "It will be playing clean into the girl's hands if she has any…"'

'That's all you heard?'

'That's all…' Sophia nodded. 'I don't know what she meant.'

'Then I believe I can enlighten you,' he said silkily. 'The sentence ended, "if she has any designs on you…" But of course you haven't, have you?' he added, tongue-in-cheek.

Feeling herself start to blush once more, she said, 'No, I haven't. Certainly not!'

Then, realizing she'd spoken much too vehemently and wishing she'd ignored his teasing, she blushed even harder.

His dark grey eyes on her face, he remarked mockingly, 'Just the bare idea seems to have made you go all hot and bothered.'

Well aware that he was laughing at her, and certain now that the Marquise and he were lovers, Sophia gathered herself and said as coolly as possible, 'I'm afraid I've already wasted too much of your time, but I'd be grateful if you could just take me to the Venice Tourist Bureau…'

'Why are you still determined not to stay at the Palazzo? Surely you're not allowing Gina's animosity to upset you?'

'No, no…not really…I'd just feel more comfortable in a hotel.'

'Rubbish. You're attaching far too much importance to what was merely a jealous outburst.'

'Whatever you call it, it's plain she doesn't want me there.'

Her conclusion that he and the Marquise were lovers was shaken when he reminded her with a touch of arrogance, 'As own Ca' Fortuna, what Gina wants or doesn't want is quite irrelevant.'

Grey eyes holding green, he added, 'I decide whom to invite…'

His handsome face was only inches away and his effect on her was overwhelming.

'I-I'm sorry,' Sophia stammered, her eyes falling beneath his.

'I've asked you to be my guest, and I'm hoping very much that you'll accept my invitation.'

She took a deep breath and nerved herself to look up. 'Thank you. I'd really like to stay.'

'Good. Though it almost took thumbscrews to get the right response.'

He leaned forward and kissed her lightly on the mouth, before getting to his feet and moving to sit behind the wheel.

CHAPTER FOUR

WHILE Sophia remained transfixed, still feeling the touch of his lips against hers, the engine coughed and spluttered into life.

A moment later they were threading their way down the canal, the water green and opaque where the low evening sun slanted across it, almost black in the deep shadows.

Her entire being, her very soul, had responded to the touch of his lips and, though his kiss had been brief, almost experimental, nothing she had ever experienced had moved her more. She would never be the same again.

She could only hope and pray Stephen hadn't noticed her reaction to what he no doubt regarded as a casual caress, while she recognized it as a catalyst that would change her life for ever.

That recognition, coupled with what had gone before, threw her into a state of emotional turmoil.

Face to face with her own vulnerability, she wondered if she had done the right thing by agreeing to stay at the Palazzo.

Even though the Marquise no longer lived there, the woman's obvious jealousy seemed to indicate that she and Stephen were lovers.

But, if they were, why had he been so keen to have *her* there? Surely he wouldn't have risked upsetting the Marquise if he cared about her?

Or did he *want* to make her jealous? Some men liked the feeling of power it gave them, enjoyed having the upper hand in a relationship, especially a clandestine one.

Sophia sighed. Although she was certain she was falling in love with him, she didn't really *know* him, know what kind of man he was, what he was capable of...

As they threaded their way through a series of narrow canals, she struggled with a jumble of disturbing thoughts and feelings.

She had only been with him for a short time, but already she felt as if she'd been put through an emotional wringer.

Though it was her own fault, she acknowledged wryly. One way or another she had made a complete fool of herself. Firstly over the hotel booking, and then over her reluctance to accept his invitation to stay at the Palazzo.

She had as good as laid bare her feelings and exposed her weaknesses. It was no wonder he had laughed at her...

If only she had taken David's advice and ignored the Marquise, things might well have been different.

Though if they *had* been different, Stephen wouldn't have kissed her, and that kiss was infinitely precious to her.

But why had he kissed her? Had it been premeditated or a spur-of-the-moment impulse? A genuine attraction or merely a light flirtation?

Impossible to tell.

She could only hope and pray it was genuine attraction...

They were on the point of rejoining the Grand Canal by the time she had managed to push aside the confusion of thoughts and start to enjoy the sights and sounds of Venice once more.

'That's better,' Stephen commented, making it clear that he'd been keeping an eye on her. 'You were looking quite fraught. I was beginning to wonder if my kissing you had seriously upset you.'

She glanced at him. He was looking straight ahead now, his profile clear-cut and handsome, the breeze of their passing ruffling his fair hair and flicking a lock across his forehead.

'No, it wasn't that,' she denied.

'Then what was it?'

With a sigh, she admitted, 'I realized I'd been behaving like a fool… I mean with regard to staying at the Palazzo.'

He raised his eyebrows. 'Wonder of wonders! An honest woman.'

'That's a very chauvinistic remark,' she said with some severity.

'But a true one, don't you think?'

'Why should women be any less honest than men?'

'That's a good question. But most of the women I've known have been anything but honest.'

'Then you must have been associating with the wrong kind of women.' The retort was out before she could prevent it.

He grimaced. 'And my mother warned me against that very thing!'

She laughed in spite of herself. 'Wonder of wonders! A man with a sense of humour.'

As soon as the words were spoken, she wished them unsaid. She had caused him enough aggravation without deliberately rubbing him up the wrong way.

But with an appreciative grin, he made the gesture of a fencer acknowledging a hit. 'Touché.'

After perhaps another hundred yards, he slowed their speed and pointed. 'We're just coming up to the Palazzo del Fortuna.'

The Palazzo, its ornate Gothic façade fronting on to the Grand Canal, stood at a junction, a narrower canal running at right angles along one side.

With its intricate lace-like balconies and delicate marble arches supported by pillars, it was one of the most beautiful buildings Sophia had ever set eyes on.

'Do you like it?' he queried.

'I think it's absolutely wonderful,' she said sincerely. 'How old is it?'

He looked pleased and, a note of pride in his voice, told her, 'It was built for Giovanni Fortuna in the early fourteen hundreds by Milanese craftsmen and stonemasons.

'Though there have been quite a few additions and alterations over the years, the façade is pure fifteenth century and one of the finest in Venice.'

'I can quite believe it.'

'The main entrance is especially fine…'

As they drew level, Sophia could see what he meant.

Beyond the stone landing stage, a short flight of elegant marble steps led up to an imposing recessed portal flanked by pale marble pillars.

'Unfortunately it's little used these days,' Stephen went on, 'though I have plans to open it up for special occasions.'

Over the doorway was what appeared to be a family coat of arms. Against a blue background was a golden lion and a white unicorn divided by a curved red shield. Above the shield ran a single word—Fortuna.

Sophia was seized by an unaccountable conviction that she had seen it before.

As she stared, a tremor of excitement running through her, his eyes fixed on her face, Stephen asked, 'Something wrong?'

'No… No… Nothing's wrong… It's just that the coat of arms over the doorway looks familiar. I feel as if I've seen it before, as if I recognize it.'

For a moment he stared at her, his eyes narrowed against the low sun, before suggesting, 'You might well have seen it in a photograph or a painting, or even in a magazine. A few years ago *Past and Present* did a feature on the Palazzo.'

'That's probably it.'

But somehow she couldn't believe that was the right answer and after a moment she identified what was wrong with it.

What she felt was not merely *recognition*. A half buried memory insisted that she had seen the coat of arms from a boat in similar circumstances—that she had been here before.

But of course she couldn't have been.

It had to be déjà vu.

When she said no more, Stephen revved the boat's engine and they turned into the side canal.

Set in the Palazzo's ornate wall, about four feet above the water, was a series of long arched windows and, on the floor above them, a recessed balcony with thin pillars and intricate stonework.

'Further down there—' Stephen pointed '—where the *fondamenta* starts, is the south entrance.'

'How many entrances are there?' she asked as they passed between huge wooden doors into the boathouse. Sunlight didn't penetrate its depths and the wash from passing traffic made the dark water heave and slop a little, like a cup of black coffee in an unsteady hand.

'Five if you include the garden,' he answered, 'but, because we usually travel by water, this is the one most used.'

He secured the boat to one of the mooring rings and vaulting lightly on to the stone landing stage, offered a hand to help her out.

As always, his touch sent a quiver running through her and made her heart beat faster.

From the landing stage several wide but shallow stone steps led up to a pair of black studded doors with a large ornate-metal lock and an old-fashioned iron bell-pull.

On the right, with a modern Yale-type lock, was a smaller door. It opened at their approach and a short sturdy-looking man wearing dark trousers and an open-necked shirt appeared.

A nice-looking man with thick white hair and heavy black brows, he put her in mind of the visitor old Mrs Caldwell had described.

'*Ciao,* Roberto,' Stephen said easily. 'This is Signorina Jordan…'

In answer to Sophia's smile, Roberto gave her a respectful nod.

'Perhaps you'll get one of the men to bring her luggage in?'

As Roberto moved to do his bidding, Stephen ushered Sophia into a large flagged hall with a massive stone fireplace at either end. It was furnished with a long table and benches and heavy old-fashioned sideboards and settles.

'As you may have gathered, this is the servants' wing,' he told her. 'At one time a small army of family retainers lived here, but these days there's scarcely more than a dozen.'

Having crossed the hall, they reached an area where on one side a stone staircase climbed to the next storey and, on the other, several arched passageways branched off.

Sophia was just wondering where they all led when Stephen told her, 'The archway we're passing now leads to the south entrance, and through here is the main hall.'

The hall was frankly magnificent. Made all of pale polished marble, its main portal was guarded by ranks of fluted columns. Crystal chandeliers hung on gold chains from the ornate ceiling and, in the centre, a graceful sweep of staircase curved upwards, while long gilt-framed mirrors lined the walls, reflecting back its splendour.

Once again Sophia got the eerie feeling that it was familiar to her, that she had seen it before. Had *been* here before.

'And this is the ballroom.'

The adjoining ballroom was equally magnificent.

'I hadn't expected anything quite this grand,' she remarked in awe.

'You should really see it at night when there's a ball in progress.'

'You've seen it like that?' she asked as they returned to the hall.

'Yes, a couple of times. Once when I was a child and I crept out of my room to sneak a look, and again on my twenty-first birthday, when Aunt Fran gave a ball in my honour.

'Then the Palazzo was full of light and colour, voices and music and movement. The whole place came to life, and it was easy to appreciate what Venetian society must have been like in its heyday.'

'It sounds magical. I'd love to see it like that.'

'Then you shall. It's my aunt's birthday at the beginning of March, so at *Carnevale* I'm hoping to give a ball in her memory.'

'When exactly is carnival time?'

'On the run up to Lent…'

Surely he wasn't expecting her to still be in Venice at Lent?

'It lasts about ten days, and everyone wears a costume of some kind and carries a mask. The celebrations culminate on Shrove Tuesday with a masked ball, a procession of boats going down the candlelit Grand Canal and a massive firework display over San Marco harbour…'

He broke off as a short, neatly dressed woman with bright black eyes and thick iron-grey hair taken back into a bun came hurrying up and gave them a smile of welcome

Speaking in Italian, he said, 'Sophia, my dear, may I introduce my housekeeper, Rosa Ponti? She and her husband Roberto practically run the Palazzo between them, and have done for more than thirty years.

'Rosa, this is Signorina Jordan…'

Rosa beamed and said, 'Welcome to Ca' Fortuna, Signorina Jordan. Your suite is all ready for you. If you would like to follow me?'

'That's all right, Rosa,' Stephen broke in crisply. 'I'll show the *signorina* round first.'

'Very well, Signor Stefano. Will you want dinner at the usual time?'

Addressing Sophia, Stephen queried, 'Would you prefer to eat out?'

'Well, I…' A little thrown by being deferred to, and uncertain what *he* would prefer, she hesitated.

'As it's your first visit I thought you might be keen to see something of Venice by night.'

Her face eager, she admitted, 'Yes, I am… If it won't upset the household arrangements?'

Turning to Rosa, Stephen said, 'Perhaps you'll be kind enough to let Angelo know that we'll be eating out this evening?'

'Of course, Signor Stefano.'

'Angelo is Rosa's son,' Stephen explained. 'A strapping lad of nearly six foot, he's the best chef in Venice.'

Rosa looked pleased. Then to Sophia, she said, 'If you would care for any help with your unpacking, please let me know and I'll send a maid along.'

'*Grazie*, Rosa.' Sophia thanked her with a smile.

Returning the smile, the small upright figure hurried away.

A hand at Sophia's waist, Stephen suggested, 'Before we go, would you like just a brief tour of Ca' Fortuna to get you orientated?'

'Oh, yes, please…'

'We'll start with the grand bits, shall we?'

As he escorted her up the elegant sweep of staircase to a wide marble landing, she voiced the query that had lodged in her mind. 'How did your housekeeper know I was staying at the Palazzo?'

The hesitation was barely noticeable before he answered easily, 'I asked her to get a room ready just in case there were any problems.'

Before she could ask any further questions, he changed the subject by remarking, 'This is the original staircase, and one of the finest still in existence.

'Once the Ca' d'Oro had finer, but in the nineteenth century the world famous ballet dancer Maria Taglioni, who had been given the palace by the Russian Prince Alexander Troubetskoy, had them ripped out along with the street portal and much of the beautiful marblework.

'Luckily the Fortuna family who lived here over the centuries valued what they had, so very little was altered.

'These are the main staterooms…' As they proceeded down a wide corridor, he opened several doors to show a series of handsome rooms with lofty ceilings and elaborate furniture.

'To the left is the long gallery, where the family portraits are hung, but I think it would be best to leave that until tomorrow.'

He escorted her through an impressive archway to a kind of inner lobby, with several doors leading off.

'At one time the family occupied this part of the house, but when Uncle Paolo became something of an invalid and couldn't manage the stairs, the living quarters were moved to the ground floor.

'Which in some ways is a pity, as the living-room on this floor, though more formal, is quite beautiful…' He paused, then laughed. 'But, having said that, the modernized living area proved to be a great deal more comfortable and practical for all concerned, especially Paolo.'

'Your uncle isn't…?'

'Still alive? No, he died about eighteen months before Aunt Fran.'

Glancing at his watch, he went on, 'We'd best get moving. You'll see this part tomorrow when you take a look at the paintings.'

Turning, he led the way through an archway opposite,

where, from an oak landing, another flight of stairs ran down to a spacious wood-panelled hall.

As they descended the stairs, he explained, 'When the ground floor was being modernized, this somewhat more convenient staircase was put in.'

Crossing the hall, he opened a pair of large ornately carved doors. 'The family accommodation is through here... As you can see, it's been arranged so that the main rooms overlook, and some have wheelchair access to, the courtyard and garden.'

The family accommodation consisted of two adjoining *en suite* bedrooms, a businesslike study, a dining-room, a morning room and a wood-panelled living-room with long windows and French windows.

Beautifully proportioned and furnished with a comfortable-looking natural leather suite and glowing antiques, the living-room was pleasant and spacious.

A rose-patterned carpet, bookcases, family photographs and a cosy fireplace with a sheepskin rug in front of the flower-filled hearth gave it a homely, lived-in feel.

Seeing her eyes fixed on the fireplace, Stephen remarked with a smile, 'Though we have central heating, as far as I'm concerned, in the winter a log fire is a must.'

'Just at the moment I find it hard to believe it can ever get cold here.'

'That's understandable. But I assure you it can get very damp and chilly when the sea fogs roll in... Now, through here is your suite...'

He led the way across the room to where a communicating door opened into another spacious and attractive sitting-room, with a thick pile carpet, comfortable armchairs and a polished writing desk.

Opposite a large stone fireplace, French windows, partially screened by hanging vines, gave on to the flagged courtyard.

Through an archway was an *en suite* bedroom dominated by a handsome four-poster with a dark blue canopy. In one corner there was a ornate black and gold lacquered chest and in the other a matching oriental screen.

Glancing around, Sophia saw that her luggage had been brought in and placed on a rack.

Following her gaze, Stephen suggested, 'If you'd like to change and freshen up before we go out?'

'Yes, I would, please.'

'Will fifteen minutes be enough?'

'Plenty, thank you.'

As soon as the door had closed behind him, she opened her case and found fresh knickers, a silky shift in a silvery olive-green, strappy sandals and a matching bag.

Then, laying them out neatly on the bed, alongside her night things, she took her sponge bag and hurried into the peach-tiled bathroom to shower.

Happiness and excitement flooding through her, she thought how lucky she was. Instead of staying in an impersonal hotel, she was in a lovely suite here in the Palazzo, right next door to Stephen.

After a moment that thought, coupled with the memory of his kiss, sounded a warning bell.

She had no defences against him, and she knew it.

Though wasn't it rather arrogant of her to presume she would need any?

Even if he wasn't already having an affair with the Marquise, it was clear that, husband or no husband, she would be more than willing. So why should he have designs on *her*?

Unless he happened to be a Casanova who felt the need to try to seduce every nubile woman who crossed his path. And, if he *was*, he wasn't the man for her.

But suppose he wasn't a Casanova? Suppose he was just a normal red-blooded man who happened to find her attractive?

Though knowing full well that he was wealthy and their life-styles were entirely different, because he was like the man in her portrait and fate had seemed to throw them together, she had come to Venice with hopes of at least trying to 'fight for him'. But, now she had seen his family background, the futility of her hopes was only too apparent.

She was right out of his class. Any idea that he might come to love her and want them to be together always was nothing but a pipedream.

If he wanted anything at all, it would just be a fling, a casual affair, and, with the Marquise clearly available, even that was unlikely.

In any case, affairs weren't her style. As far as she was concerned, sex and love went hand in hand and called for the commitment of marriage.

That being so, she must try to give up all thoughts of romance, stay calm and unmoved and concentrate solely on the job she had come here to do.

But, as someone had once said, hope sprang eternal, and there was no way she could prevent herself from *hoping* that fate intended them to be together.

Showered and dried, she cleaned her teeth, brushed her long dark hair and, leaving it to curl loosely around her shoulders, pulled on her clothes and applied a light touch of make-up.

Finding her jewellery box, she took out the pearl drop earrings her father had bought her for her twenty-first birthday and was just fastening them to her neat lobes when she heard Stephen's knock.

Putting the box back in the top of her case, she picked up her bag and hurried to open the door.

At the sight of him her mouth went dry.

He was freshly shaven and his thick fair hair, still a little damp from the shower, was trying to curl. Wearing a well-cut dinner jacket and a black-bow tie, he looked dangerously handsome and virile.

'All set?'

She nodded.

He ran an appreciative eye over her slender figure and, smiling down at her, said, 'You look delightful. I like your hair loose…'

As he spoke he took a silky strand and twined it around his finger, holding her captive for a moment while he watched her face.

When she started to blush, he let it spring loose and asked, 'Now, shall I call a water-taxi or would you prefer to walk?'

Collecting herself, she answered, 'I'd much prefer to walk.'

His approving glance confirming she'd made the right choice, he said, 'Then let's go,' and led her across the living-room and through long, elegant French windows into the courtyard.

It was a lovely evening, clear and calm, a thin sickle moon hanging in the east, the western sky mottled with pink and gold and the palest of duck-egg blues. With the setting of the sun the fierce heat had died, leaving the air soft and balmy.

A wing of the building ran down either side of the paved courtyard, and in the centre was an old stone well covered by a heavy metal grille.

There were an abundance of green creepers and bright tubs of flowers, and a table and chairs and some comfortable-looking loungers were grouped beneath a trellis-work of vines.

Sophia thought how pleasant it must be to sit out here in the heat of the day.

Beyond the courtyard, enclosed by a high stone wall, the garden was green and lush, shaded by trees and fragrant with flowering shrubs and plants. From a sunken area overhung with ferns, mossy paths led off to secret arbours and hidden fountains splashed and played.

As they strolled along a tree-bordered path beneath a lacy

green canopy of leaves, he took her hand and tucked it companionably through his arm.

The feel of his muscular arm through the thin material of his jacket sent her heart racing like a mad thing, making nonsense of her decision to stay calm and unmoved.

Her heart rate had just slowed to somewhere near normal when, to the left, she noticed the remains of two ivy-entwined marble columns rising from the cover of some glossy-leaved ground plants.

As, fascinated, she paused to look closer, Stephen explained, 'Ca' Fortuna was built on the site of a Byzantine palace, and these pillars were part of the original portal...'

'That's wonderful!' she exclaimed.

'If you're interested, some time I'll show you the remains of the mosaic flooring that's been preserved inside the walls of the east wing.'

'Oh, yes, please. If I hadn't chosen to take art, I would have liked to have studied archaeology.' Sophia's eyes lit up.

Stephen smiled down at her, pleased by her enthusiasm. 'Then we have a lot in common. Had I been free to follow my own inclinations, I would have studied human history and prehistory with a view to becoming an archaeologist.

'As it was, I was expected to do my filial duty and take over the business empire that my father and grandfather had built up, so I took psychology, statistics and economics...' As his voice trailed off his expression became guarded.

Until then Sophie had thought of Stephen as being lucky. But now, perhaps for the first time, she realized that family wealth could bring its own burden of restrictions and responsibilities.

As though reading her mind, he added emphatically, 'However, as I'm one of the fortunate people of this world, I have to be thankful.'

When they reached the far end of the garden, Stephen felt

in his jacket pocket and producing a bunch of keys, selected one and opened a stout gate set in the high wall.

The gate gave on to a quiet *campo* dominated by an old church with big black studded doors. To the right, a narrow *calle* disappeared between tall buildings with grey-shuttered windows, and to the left, beyond the *fondamenta*, the canal ran past, spanned by an ornate metal bridge.

'Now, before we decide exactly which way to go, have you any particular desires or wishes?'

She had no difficulty choosing. 'I'd like to see the Piazza San Marco, if possible.'

'Exactly what I had in mind. I thought, if you were agreeable, that we might start with an aperitif at Florians. Then a short distance away is the Rizanti, one of my favourite restaurants. It's quiet and select and the food, especially the seafood, is out of this world.'

'That sounds wonderful.'

Smiling at her enthusiasm, he took her hand once more and said, 'Then our most interesting route will be across the bridge.'

As they approached the canal where, on their left, three shallow steps ran down to the water, he remarked, 'This is the Rio Castagnio. When I was young I had many a scolding for sneaking out of the house to swim here…'

While, hand in hand, almost as if they were lovers, they wended their way south towards San Marco, he told her amusing stories of his early childhood.

As they walked, a blue velvet, star-embroidered cloak of dusk began to settle over the city. Lights started to appear everywhere, shining and sparkling like multicoloured jewels.

Venice by night was a magical place full of life and movement and colour and, while Stephen remained silent and watched her face, Sophia absorbed the sights and sounds and smells with the utmost delight.

Candlelit tables beneath colourful umbrellas, tubs of flowers and strings of lanterns, dark water and bright reflections broken up by ripples, oars splashing, an accordion playing, talk and laughter, a gondolier serenading his passengers and, mingling with the salt tang of the sea, the scent of food and wine, perfume and coffee, brandy and tobacco smoke.

When they reached the Piazza San Marco, its lamplit arcades were still teeming with people taking an evening stroll and its café tables were busy.

On the far side of the square an orchestra was playing Gershwin, and closer at hand she could hear the haunting strains of Ravel's Bolero.

Having expected so much, Sophia had been afraid she might be disappointed. But, with its sheer scale and intriguing blend of Eastern and Western architecture, its famous Clock Tower and soaring Campanile, and the domes of St Mark's Basilica forming an exotic backdrop, it was all she had imagined and more.

For several minutes she stood soaking up the atmosphere, silent and absorbed.

'Well?' Stephen asked at last.

Lifting shining eyes, she said, 'It has to be one of the most beautiful squares in the world.'

'It's certainly one of the most intriguing,' he agreed as he led her over to Florians and seated her at a vacant table. 'Over the centuries it's been the setting for bullfights and pig hunts, pageants and processions, carnivals and feast days, and of course it always has been, and still is, the heart and soul of the city—'

He broke off and asked, 'What would you like?' as a black-tied waiter appeared to take their order.

When she hesitated, he suggested, 'A gin and tonic, perhaps? Or a Manhattan?'

She shook her head. 'I don't really like spirits.'

'Then what's it to be?'

'A glass of dry white wine, please.'

'A glass of Verdicchio and a Campari soda.'

Their order given, the waiter glided away, to return quite quickly with their drinks on a round silver tray balanced on one raised palm.

Served in a tall narrow glass, the wine was clear and pale with a faint greenish cast.

'Try it and see what you think,' Stephen said. 'I'll order something else if you find it's not to your taste.'

She obeyed and found it was crisp and cool, full of delicate flavour. 'It's lovely,' she told him.

'Sure?'

'Quite sure. Try some.' She offered him the glass.

Instead of accepting it, he leaned forward a little and left her to tilt it against his parted lips.

As he took a sip, their eyes met over the glass and once more soft wings fluttered in her stomach.

Her voice not quite steady, she asked, 'Don't you think it's lovely?'

His eyes on her face, he agreed, 'Lovely, indeed.'

There was no doubt as to his meaning and she found herself blushing as, flustered by his unwavering regard, she looked hastily away.

She heard his soft, satisfied laugh.

Clearly he found it amusing to tease her and she told herself vexedly that she would have to find some armour against him. Otherwise she would be in a perpetual state of turmoil.

Afraid to look at him until she had regained her composure, while she sipped her wine she listened to the music and, against a spectacular background that put her in mind of a lavish film set, watched the evening *passaggiata*.

All human life was there. Young couples strolling arm in arm, elderly couples holding hands, teenage lovers twined around each other, family parties of parents and older children chattering away like magpies, one or two well-dressed elderly men who had the air of Venetian patricians, and camera-slung tourists still wearing T-shirts and shorts.

Eventually, satisfied that she was mistress of herself once more, she remarked, 'I don't wonder you love Venice. It must be hard to leave it.'

'Let's say I'm glad to be back… Now, would you like another glass of wine or are you ready to eat?'

'I'm ready to eat, if you are.'

He rose to his feet and pulled out her chair. 'Then let's go. Carlo will be expecting us.'

CHAPTER FIVE

THEY left the square through an archway under the Torre dell'Orologio and after a short distance turned down a *calle* which led to a small *campo* with a canal running down one side. Overlooking the canal was the terrace of the Rizanti, its candlelit tables crowded with people.

Once inside the restaurant they were greeted by a nice-looking man with dark crinkly hair, wearing impeccable evening clothes.

'Stefano... It's good to see you.'

'And you, Carlo.'

The two men shook hands warmly.

Putting an arm around Sophia's waist, Stephen went on, '*Cara mia,* I'd like to introduce my old friend, Carlo Verdi... Carlo, this is Sophia Jordan, the special lady I told you about.'

Wondering at the way Stephen had phrased the introduction, Sophia smiled and murmured a polite, 'How do you do?'

Bowled over by that smile, Carlo took her proffered hand and raised it to his lips. 'I'm delighted to meet you, Signorina Jordan... If I may say so, you are even more beautiful than Stefano told me...'

The knowledge that Stephen thought her beautiful made Sophia colour with a mixture of pleasure and self-consciousness.

Turning to the other man, Carlo clapped him on the shoulder. 'My felicitations. You're a very lucky man to have found such a woman... Tonight the meal is on the house.

'Now, I have a table here for you but, as it is a little crowded, I thought perhaps you and the *signorina* might prefer to eat in the courtyard?'

Stephen gave Sophia an interrogative glance.

The restaurant was made up of a series of delightful little salons, mirrored and frescoed and carpeted in crimson. They each held no more than two or three tables, most of which were already occupied by a well-dressed clientele.

Candlelight, and crimson velvet curtains held back by gold-tasselled cords, lent the salons a charming air of intimacy. But it was such a lovely evening...

'Outside,' she said decisively.

His little nod of approval suggested that once again her choice had pleased him.

'If you like seafood...?' Carlo addressed Sophia.

'I love it.'

'Excellent! Then when you can spare time from Stefano's paintings you must come here often.'

Speaking to both of them now, he went on, 'But for the moment may I recommend tonight's special menu? I believe the chef has excelled himself.'

After an enquiring glance at Sophia, Stephen answered, 'Then we'll be happy to try it.'

'I'm sure it will be wonderful,' she said.

Carlo gave her a beaming smile and, beckoning the head waiter, issued some low-voiced instructions.

'If you will follow me?' The *maître d'* led the way through a lantern-hung courtyard with a scattering of tables to a secluded, candlelit table set beneath a canopy of vines.

As soon as they had been seated, he vanished, only to

return almost immediately with a napkin-covered trolley that held a bottle of vintage champagne in an ice bucket and two crystal flutes.

'With Signor Verdi's compliments.'

He untwisted the wire, eased out the cork with a satisfying pop and poured the smoking wine, before slipping quietly away.

'Signor Verdi seems to think it's a special occasion…' Sophia ventured.

When Stephen said nothing, she persisted, '*Why* does he? What did you tell him to make him think that?'

'I mentioned that it was your first time in Venice,' he replied smoothly.

Frowning, she asked, 'If that's all, why did he congratulate you?'

'Because I told him what I told you at A Volonté—that I'd found just the woman I needed.'

She had the strangest feeling that, though his answer was no doubt truthful as far as it went, it was in reality a sophism designed to hide the truth.

But why should he *want* to hide the truth?

Before she could speculate any further, Stephen raised his glass in a toast. 'Here's to us… May our relationship have a successful outcome.'

No doubt he meant a *working* relationship, Sophia thought as she lifted her glass and sipped the excellent champagne.

She was about to ask him how many paintings were involved, when the waiter brought their first course.

It was a fish mousse, so light and delicate it seemed a sacrilege to talk, so she fell silent and simply enjoyed it.

The second course of pasta and prawns in a delectable asparagus sauce was, if anything, even better, and the tiramisu that followed was out of this world.

Crisp, wafer-thin biscuits with creamy dolcelatte and a rich, fragrant coffee rounded off the best meal Sophia could ever remember having.

While they ate, very little had been said, and they were drinking their coffee before Stephen broke the silence to ask, 'I hope the food came up to your expectations?'

'Everything was absolutely delicious. I can't remember when I've enjoyed a meal so much.'

'Neither can I,' he admitted. 'Of course one's companion makes a lot of difference. In my opinion good food should be savoured, and it's a pleasure to dine with a woman who doesn't feel the need to talk all the time.'

She was greatly relieved that he hadn't found her quietness boring.

'So, apart from the food, what do you think of the Rizanti?'

She smiled up at him. 'It's really special. I'm not surprised that it's one of your favourite restaurants. Have you known it for a long time?'

Taking a sip of his drink he replied. 'Yes… It's a family owned business. I can remember my aunt bringing me here for a treat when I was quite a small child, and Carlo's father giving me my first sip of Chianti.'

'Did you like it?'

'I pretended to, but Aunt Fran must have guessed how I really felt, because as soon as Carlo's father had gone she gave me a sweet to take away the taste. I decided there and then that I would never drink wine when I grew up.'

Smiling, Sophia said, 'Your aunt sounds nice. What was she like?'

Stephen sat back in his seat and thought for a moment. 'Kind-hearted, good-tempered, incurably honest, businesslike when necessary, yet romantic, a dreamer of dreams. A gentle, compassionate woman—though anything but weak—a woman who gave more than she took, and loved more than she hated.

'She had a passion for books and art and music, and she played the piano extremely well. Whenever I saw her she appeared to be smiling and serene, but there was a certain sadness about her, as if life hadn't given her what she most wanted.'

Sophia found herself enchanted by his description. 'You were fond of her?'

'Very.'

'Am I right in thinking your aunt and uncle had no children of their own?'

He shook his head. 'You're wrong, as it happens. Gina is their daughter.'

'Oh…' Sophia was surprised and showed it. 'Then the Marquise is your cousin?'

'Yes.'

That explained the closeness between them, and why Gina had lived at the Palazzo.

'So presumably you played together as children?'

'Not exactly. You see there's something of an age gap, so at first Gina regarded me as a nuisance and gave me a wide berth. It was only as I grew older that, during my visits to Venice, we spent time together and really got to know one another…'

While she listened, Sophia found herself puzzling over what Stephen had just told her. If Gina was the daughter of his aunt and uncle, why hadn't *she* inherited the Palazzo…? Unless…

Watching Sophia's absorbed face, the slight frown that creased her smooth forehead, he offered, 'A penny for your thoughts.'

A little flustered, she half shook her head.

'So you won't sell, huh? Oh, well, it doesn't really matter; I can guess what you're thinking…'

When she said nothing, he went on, 'You were wondering why the Palazzo was left to me rather than to Gina… Have you reached any conclusion?'

Flushing because he had so easily read her thoughts, she demurred, 'I'm sure you must think it's none of my business.'

'If I thought that, I wouldn't be discussing it with you.'

When, his eyes fixed on her face, he waited, she found herself saying, 'I can only presume that they wanted, or family tradition demanded, a male heir.'

'It's quite true that Paolo, in particular, had hoped for a son and, if they'd had one, things might have been different... Though inheriting the Palazzo isn't contingent on being a male. Aunt Fran inherited it from her parents.'

'Oh... Then why—?' She stopped short.

He answered her unfinished question. 'In this case, it was to carry on the Fortuna blood line. You see, Paolo, who was ten years older than Aunt Fran, was a widower when they met, and Gina was the daughter of his first marriage...'

Stephen paused to refill both their coffee cups before going on. 'He was an extraordinarily handsome man and had a great deal of charm—when he cared to use it—but there was a less pleasant side to him, and he was far from easy to live with.'

'Did your aunt and her stepdaughter get on well?' Sophia asked.

'Unfortunately not. Though Aunt Fran did her best, Gina bitterly opposed her father's second marriage and hated the thought of any other woman taking her mother's place.

'In the end she made herself so obnoxious that even her father grew tired of the endless scenes and threatened to send her away to school if her behaviour didn't improve.

'On the surface things quietened down, but she blamed her stepmother for the ultimatum and her hatred and resentment grew and poisoned any possible relationship between them.

'All in all, she was an unhappy child and, young as I was, I remember feeling sorry for her.'

Sophia listened intently. 'Did matters between her and her stepmother improve as she got older?'

He shook his head. 'Not really. Fortunately the Palazzo is a big place and for most of the time she and Aunt Fran lived under the same roof they managed to avoid each other.

'On the few social occasions they were forced to meet, they were studiously polite to one another. No more, no less.

'However, with her own suite and a generous allowance, Gina was satisfied with things as they were, that is until her father first took ill.

'She was used to a life of luxury and had no intention of giving it up if she could help it. But the thought of how her situation might change if anything happened to her father worried her a good deal.

'That's why, when the Marquis d'Orsini proposed, she decided to accept him.'

'You mean she married him for his money?' Sophia recognized the shocked tone in her voice too late to mask her disapproval.

Stephen raised an eyebrow. 'I gather you don't approve?'

'I'm sorry, I shouldn't have—'

'Don't worry,' he said at once. 'A spot of honesty is like a breath of fresh air.'

Then, incisively, 'So you don't believe in marrying for money?'

Shaking her head, Sophia replied emphatically. 'No.'

'Why not?'

'Because I can't imagine it would make either partner happy.' She played with the stem of her wineglass as she revealed her thoughts, hoping Stephan wouldn't think her too judgemental.

'In this case it didn't.'

Almost sadly, he added, 'Gina might have been happy had she chosen to marry the man who, at the time, was in love with her.

'He would have done anything for her, but at that point he

was young and untried and had very little money of his own. Added to that, she knew his family disliked her and might well disown him if he went ahead and made her his wife.

'*He* would have chanced it, but *she* was afraid to, so when the marquis offered her marriage, though he was thirty-five years her senior, and a lecher to boot, she was fool enough to accept…

'At first he treated her like royalty and lavished gifts on her but, as soon as the honeymoon period was over, everything changed and he started to make her life hell…'

Hearing the bitterness in his voice, Sophia realized that, in spite of everything, Stephen *cared* about his cousin.

Gently, she said, 'I'm sorry things went badly.'

'You have a kind heart. Most people would say she'd brought it on herself. Which, in all honesty, she had. But no one deserves a life like that…'

Grimly, he went on, 'The sadistic old devil treated her as if she were a *bought* woman rather than his wife. For eight years she was forced to put up with all the indignities he heaped on her, as well as his numerous affairs.

'When he died recently, I don't think anyone could have blamed her for being relieved…'

So the Marquise was a widow.

'She had looked forward to being wealthy and to owning Ca' d'Orsini, but instead she found she had only been left a meagre allowance and the *use* of the house during her lifetime, both of those to be forfeited if she married again…'

A shade cynically, he added, 'Which means she needs another rich husband.'

'But surely after so much unhappiness—' Sophia abruptly stopped speaking.

'You mean she should have learnt her lesson? Sadly some people never do. However, she may be a great deal luckier next time.

'Tell me, Sophia—' leaning forward he studied her intently '—if you don't intend to marry for money, what will you marry for?'

Looking into the handsome face so close to hers, she was struck dumb. The candlelight picked out the planes and hollows, the well marked brows and sweep of thick blond lashes, the high cheekbones and strong nose, the chiselled mouth, with its combination of austerity and passion, and the cleft chin she longed to touch...

After a long moment he reminded her, 'You haven't answered my question.'

Unable to tear her gaze away, she whispered, 'Love,' and felt her cheeks grow warm.

'Romantic, as well as honest.'

Sensing mockery, she flashed, 'Well, if not for love, what would *you* marry for?'

Taking the wind out of her sails, he reached for her hand and held it fast. 'Though it doesn't necessarily guarantee the marriage will be successful, I believe that love, especially when combined with respect and genuine *caring*, offers by far the best chance of happiness.

'Aunt Fran thought so too, but sadly those elements were missing from her own marriage, and it proved to be far from happy.'

Wits scattered by the way his thumb was stroking over her soft palm, Sophia pulled her hand free and blurted out, 'So it wasn't just problems with her stepdaughter?'

'No... Had it been just that, I believe she would have taken it in her stride. But right from the start Paolo proved to be arrogant and uncaring.

'Then one night he got drunk and let slip the fact that he'd only married her to get his hands on the Palazzo and the price-less Padova Pearls, which had been in the family for generations.

'Armed with that knowledge, she determined to make

certain that if she died first he got neither, and she willed them both away from him.' Stephan went on. 'Realizing what a bad mistake he'd made, he swore he hadn't meant it, but when she refused to alter the will he walked out, taking Gina with him.

'After a while he came back, just briefly, to see if she'd changed her mind. Finding she hadn't, he left again, apparently for good.

'The rest of the family wanted her to divorce him, but Aunt Fran didn't believe in divorce and refused.

'Everyone thought they'd finally seen the last of him, but after about eighteen months he reappeared again and begged for a second chance.

'Very much against her family's wishes, she took him and his daughter back.

'He did his best to make amends and for a time they seemed somewhat happier. But he badly wanted a child, presumably so it could inherit the two things he coveted,' he said coldly.

'Aunt Fran wanted a child too, but when that didn't happen she accepted it as God's will.

'Paolo didn't. He blamed her, and wanted her to go for tests. When she flatly refused, he went himself to prove the point.

'But the tests indicated that it was *he* who had a problem. Since fathering Gina, he had developed a medical condition which made him unable to father any more children.

'That knowledge, rather than improving matters, seemed to make things worse, and their marriage became just a sham. He used to fly into drunken rages and break things and more than once Aunt Fran was forced to take refuge with Rosa and Roberto.

'However, because of her views on divorce, she and Paolo remained together.' Stephen raked a hand through his hair. 'But, though Aunt Fran herself must have been anything but happy, she said that, in the past, the Palazzo had always been a happy place and in the future would make a happy home for me.

'Now, because of her untimely death, I'm here a lot sooner than I'd expected.'

Sophia was fascinated by his story. 'And you're intending to stay?'

'Yes,' he said decidedly. 'Apart from an occasional trip to the States, now I have a good right-hand man I can trust implicitly, experienced managers in key positions and all the benefits of modern technology, I should be able to run things quite successfully from here.'

The news sounded like a death knell. If he was planning to live in Venice permanently, when her job here was finished it was unlikely that she would ever see him again…

'Something wrong?' His voice broke into her decidedly gloomy thoughts.

'No… No, nothing's wrong. Why do you ask?'

'You looked as if something had upset you.'

'No, of course not. I'm fine. Just a bit tired.'

Glancing at his watch, he said, 'You must be. It's later than I'd realized, and you've had a long day.'

Signalling a waiter, he asked, 'Can you rustle up a taxi?'

'Certainly, Signor Haviland.'

By the time they had thanked Carlo for his hospitality and said their goodnights, there was a water-taxi waiting alongside the steps that led down from the *fondamenta*.

As soon as Stephen had helped her in and taken a seat by her side, they were underway.

It was cooler now and the breeze of their passing made her shiver a little.

Feeling that involuntary movement, Stephen slipped out of his jacket and put it around her shoulders. It still held the warmth of his body and she breathed in the clean masculine scent of him as she held the lapels together over her chest.

Though there were still plenty of people about, some of the cafés and restaurants were starting to close and, apart from the odd gondola, the smaller canals they traversed were practically deserted.

At a junction they were held up by traffic lights, then they were off again, moving quickly, so that all Sophia could gather were fleeting impressions.

Patches of light and shade, moving shapes and shadows, a lantern's rays reflected in dark water, the door of an old boathouse with rotting wood like jagged black teeth, a cat slinking past, then the sudden gleam of its eyes as it looked at them…

'Won't be long now,' Stephen remarked.

Belatedly she recognized the canal that ran alongside the Palazzo and a moment or two later they were pulling in to the lighted boathouse.

Having helped her on to the landing stage, Stephen paid the taxi driver and wished him a cheerful, *'Buona notte.'*

As the boat revved up and departed, he turned to her and said with a grin, 'It's a shame to disturb the servants at this time of night, so stand still while I rifle your pocket for the key.'

He moved closer and began to feel in the right hand pocket of the jacket she was still wearing.

As she stood looking up at him, the breath caught in her throat, he said softly, 'If you look at me like that, you're just asking to be kissed.'

'Oh, but I—'

The words died as he took advantage of her parted lips. Though his kiss was light, this time there was nothing experimental about it. Now it was a man kissing a woman he knew *wanted* to be kissed.

After a moment or so his arms went around her and, drawing

her close, he deepened the kiss until her knees were weak, her head was spinning and her very soul was his for the taking.

Eventually he reluctantly lifted his head and, without a word, turned the key in the lock and, an arm about her shoulders, led her inside and closed the door behind them.

They crossed the servants' hall, their footsteps echoing hollowly in the stillness, and took a passageway dimly lit by wall sconces through to the family living quarters.

The blood thrumming in her veins, Sophia felt a breathless anticipation, a mixture of excitement and elation that met and matched his unspoken urgency.

When they reached the sitting-room, where several standard lamps were casting pools of golden light, still without a word being spoken, he slipped the jacket from her shoulders and tossed it aside, before taking her in his arms and starting to kiss her again.

She had waited all her life for this man, this moment, and, her customary caution deserting her, she surrendered herself, loving the feel of his mouth moving against hers and his hands travelling over her slender curves.

As though he couldn't get enough of her, while his hands learned about her body, he kissed her forehead and temples, her closed eyelids and cheeks, her jawline and neck, the warm hollow at the base of her throat and the smooth skin of her shoulders, before returning to her lips.

Drugged by the sweetness of his kisses, lost in a world of sensual delight, she lay quietly, pliantly against him, content to drift on a warm tide of joy and happiness.

It wasn't until his skilful, experienced hands began to caress her breasts, stroking and squeezing, teasing the sensitive nipples that, desire running like molten lava through her veins, she began to gasp and shudder.

After a moment his hands grew still and he drew back a little.

She opened heavy lids to find he was looking down at her assessingly.

His eyes were dark with desire and, caught up now by the rising excitement, needing more than kisses, she put her hands flat-palmed against his chest and pressed the lower half of her body against his.

With a little smile of satisfaction and triumph, he slid aside the thin straps of her dress and low-cut bra and began to ease them down her arms.

Then, bending his fair head, his lips traced the upper curves of her breasts and found the shadowy hollow between them. When they closed around one firm nipple, feeling the damp warmth of his mouth through the thin, lacy material of her bra, she started to shudder afresh.

She had almost reached the point of no return when, at the back of her mind, an alarm bell sounded, awakening common sense.

What was she *doing?*

He couldn't possibly know how strongly she felt about him. As far as *he* was concerned, they had only met a few days ago. If she was weak enough to go to bed with him so soon, what would he think of her?

He would think she was cheap, easy, any man's for the taking.

As well as losing her heart, she had come perilously close to losing her head and, along with it, her pride and self-respect.

The realization was like a douche of cold water.

She jerked herself free and, pulling up the straps of her bra and dress, stammered, 'I-I'm sorry… Really sorry… But I *can't* go to bed with you…'

'You mean…?'

Incurably honest, she answered without considering the consequences. 'No, it's not that. I…'

His grey eyes narrowed. 'Then why can't you? You told me there was no other man in your life.'

'There isn't.'

'So what's the problem?'

The problem was she had suddenly found herself in too deep. If she had been thinking, she would never have let things go so far. But she hadn't been thinking, only feeling.

Reaching out, he pulled her close and, holding her fast, lifted her face up to his.

'Don't kiss me again…' she cried.

He kissed her lightly, teasingly, and his lips lingering at the corner of her mouth, asked, 'Why shouldn't I kiss you?'

'Because I don't want you to,' she croaked.

'Liar. You *do* want me to kiss you.' His voice dropping to a whisper, he went on, 'Don't try to tell me that this attraction isn't mutual.

'You want the same things that I do. To go to bed and make long, delectable love, then sleep in my arms until we waken and make love again.'

'Please, Stephen…' she begged huskily, terrified of weakening.

'Tell me the truth,' he insisted.

She took a deep shaky breath and pulled herself free. 'I *don't* want to sleep with you.'

'Yet seconds ago you pressed yourself against me, wanting nothing more than my kisses?'

'No. I mean yes, I was but…' She started to get flustered, unsure how to answer him.

'Tell me why you've changed your mind.'

Miserably, she blurted out, 'We don't really know one another.'

'I know all I need to know. In any case, wouldn't you call sleeping together getting to know one another? At least in the biblical sense.'

'I don't want to sleep with you,' she repeated jerkily.

His jaw tightened, but his voice was quiet and even as he asked, 'Sophie, tell me why not…'

Wanting to back away, she somehow stood her ground. She had led him on and if he was angry she could hardly blame him.

'It's too soon,' she said helplessly.

'So what is the standard probationary period that your conquests have to serve?' he questioned ruthlessly.

Flushing, she denied, 'I haven't had a string of conquests, or lovers. I'm not that kind of woman. I've never…'

For a moment she considered trying to make him understand. Then, giving up, she turned and fled into her own suite.

Closing the door behind her, she stood in the dark with her back to the panels, churned up and wretched, shaking all over.

She'd done the right thing, of course she had.

Then why did she feel so bitterly unhappy?

Who was she trying to kid? She knew quite well why. Because she *wanted* to be with him. *Wanted* to be in his arms, in his bed.

He was the only man she had ever really loved, *would* ever love, and even if his interest was short-lived she wanted that time with him. Wanted the memories to keep and to cherish.

But now it was too late. For the sake of her pride, and that was all it amounted to, she had rejected him, angered him, run away.

He was hardly likely to forgive her. From now on, no doubt he would be cool and distant. Their relationship would be purely business.

If only she had taken things more slowly, it could have been so different. Her first day in Venice could have ended happily, with sweet dreams, tomorrow to look forward to and high hopes for the future…

Instead it had ended badly, with anger and misery and frustration, any hopes she might have cherished dashed to the ground.

She wanted to cry.

But what was the use of crying? It would solve absolutely nothing.

Making an effort to pull herself together, she felt for the light switch and pressed it. There was a click, but no lights came on.

Frowning a little, she flicked it on and off.

Still nothing.

Though there were deep shadows, the night wasn't entirely black and she was able to find her way safely across the room and through the archway into her bedroom.

But, once again, when she pressed the switch, the lights refused to work.

There had been lights on in other parts of the Palazzo, so perhaps this suite was on a different circuit and a fuse had blown?

But, after what had happened, there was no way she could go back to ask for Stephen's help.

Trying to quell a growing feeling of unease, she told herself firmly that tomorrow she would mention it to the housekeeper, but in the meantime she would manage somehow.

Leaving the bathroom door open to let in what faint light there was she creamed off her make-up, cleaned her teeth and brushed her hair before pulling on her ivory satin nightdress.

She was about to get into bed when, realizing she was still wearing her earrings, she lifted the lid of her case and felt for her jewellery box.

It was a shock to find that it was no longer there, and surely she hadn't left her things in such disorder? No, of course she hadn't.

Someone must have searched through her case and stolen her box.

But, even as the frantic thought crossed her mind, her fingers came into contact with the solid domed lid and she breathed a sigh of relief.

Though the box wasn't where she had left it, it was still there, thank the Lord, partially buried under the rest of her belongings.

Whoever had searched though her case must have been disturbed, leaving everything in such a muddle.

But who could it have been?

Not a thief. Nothing had been taken.

A nosy servant, perhaps?

It seemed unlikely. But what other explanation could there possibly be?

A new thought occurred to her and she wondered—was it possible that this was in anyway connected with her semi-conviction that someone had searched through her flat?

No! The notion was ludicrous. A London flat and a Venetian Palazzo were worlds apart. And the bare idea that she might have something someone wanted badly enough to follow her to Venice for took the whole thing into the realms of fantasy.

With a sigh, she put her earrings in the box and replaced it. Then, climbing into the four-poster, she pulled up the light-weight duvet and closed her eyes.

CHAPTER SIX

BUT while her body was comfortable, her mind wasn't, and after a minute or so, unable to sleep for the unhappy thoughts that kept churning round and round in her brain, she opened her eyes again and lay staring blindly into the darkness.

What was that?

Somewhere in the deep shadows of the far corner, close to the oriental screen, she sensed, rather than saw, a movement.

A chill of fear ran through her. Sitting bolt upright, she demanded sharply, 'Who's there?'

There was no response, just utter stillness.

Though what had she expected?

Of course there was no one there. Just because she was upset, she was letting her nerves get the better of her, acting like a complete idiot.

She was about to lie down again when she became convinced that—almost blending into the silence but not quite—she could hear the faint, rasping whisper of someone breathing.

The fine hairs on the back of her neck rose and her skin goosefleshed.

Unconsciously holding her breath, she listened.

Not a sound.

She was just tired and tense, and obviously getting paranoid, she told herself crossly.

All the same, before she could make any further attempt to sleep, she would have to get up and check, if only to set her mind at rest.

Gritting her teeth, she swung her feet to the floor and started for the corner. She had only taken a few steps when a man's dark shape detached itself from the surrounding darkness and lunged at her.

Shock tore a scream from her throat.

He pushed her roughly aside, catching her shoulder a glancing blow that sent her sprawling, momentarily winding her.

As she struggled for breath she heard the sound of a door being thrown open and Stephen came through the archway.

Striding over, he crouched by her side and, an arm beneath her shoulders, helped her to sit up. 'Are you all right?' he asked urgently. 'Were you hurt?'

Though some light was shining in through the door he'd left open, it was still too dark to see the expression on his face but she could tell he was deeply concerned.

'No… I'm all right,' she managed.

'Sure?'

'Quite sure… Just a bit winded.'

He helped her up and, steering her to the nearest chair, ordered, 'Stay there a minute,' and vanished into the gloom.

By the time he returned, shock had set in and she was cold inside and shaking like a leaf.

With a muttered, 'Hell!' he gathered her into his arms and, carrying her through to his living-room, put her down on the couch and settled some cushions behind her.

Looking down at her, he thought he had never seen anything more beautiful. Her face was innocent of make-up and slightly shiny and, with her dark silky hair tumbling round her shoulders and her green-gold eyes too big for her pale face, she looked defenceless, vulnerable.

Noticing how she was having to bite her bottom lip to stop it trembling, he said remorsefully, 'I'm a fool. I should never have left you.'

'I'm all right, really I am,' she assured him shakily.

He took her hand and, finding it icy cold, commented grimly, 'You're as white as a ghost and your hands are like ice.'

He disappeared into his bedroom to return almost immediately with a soft lightweight rug, which he tucked around her.

Then, from the oak sideboard, he collected a decanter of brandy and two goblets and, putting them on the coffee table, proceeded to pour a generous measure of the amber liquid into one of the glasses.

Passing it to her carefully, he instructed, 'Sip that slowly.'

She was still shaking so much that the glass clinked against her teeth and at first she was forced to use both hands to hold it steady before she could manage to drink.

As she sipped, shuddering from time to time as the strong spirit hit the back of her throat, her inward coldness eased and the trembling gradually ceased.

Noting the change, he took her free hand and observed approvingly, 'That's better... Your hands are warmer and your colour's coming back...'

For the first time she registered fully that he was barefoot and wearing a short navy-blue silk dressing gown belted around his lean waist.

His fair hair was rumpled and still slightly damp, as though he had just stepped from the shower before he'd responded to her cry...

At that instant there was a knock at the door and she jumped.

'It's all right,' he said reassuringly. 'It'll be Roberto to report on what they found.'

Letting go of her hand, he padded to the door and opened it, then stood for a while in low-toned conversation, before saying, '*Va bene... Grazie,* Roberto...' Then, 'Yes, two should be enough... No, there's no need. The rest of you can get back to bed. *Buona notte.*'

Returning to the hearth, he took her glass and, adding another dash of brandy, told her firmly, 'Before you think of protesting, it's strictly for medicinal purposes.'

She accepted it meekly and watched as he poured a measure for himself.

Cradling his own goblet between his palms, he sat down again and observed carefully, 'Now, as you've suffered a bad fright, and I think it's preferable to get this kind of thing out of one's system, I suggest you tell me exactly what happened after you left me.'

Dragging her eyes away from the tanned column of his throat and the smooth expanse of chest revealed by the gaping revers of his dressing gown, she obeyed. 'I found the lights in my living-room wouldn't come on and, when I went through, the bedroom lights wouldn't work either...

'I thought there must be a fuse gone, so I started to get ready for bed. When I wanted to put my earrings away I discovered that my jewellery box had been moved and someone had searched through my case—'

'Was anything missing?' he asked quickly.

'Not that I'm aware of.'

His legs, she noticed, were straight and muscular, lightly sprinkled with golden hair, his bare feet long and well-shaped, with neat toes...

'You must have been alarmed at that point?'

Lassoing her straying attention, she agreed, 'I was, a little... But I thought perhaps some—' she hesitated, then went on '—some servant had looked through it.'

He frowned. 'Then what did you do?'

'I got into bed, but I couldn't settle… I thought I saw a movement in the far corner by the screen, then I heard a faint sound, like someone with asthma trying to breathe quietly.

'I knew I wouldn't be able to sleep until I'd made sure no one was there, so I—'

'Why didn't you call me?' he demanded. Then, quickly, 'Silly question… Go on.'

Looking anywhere but at him, she continued, 'I got out of bed and was going towards the corner when this figure suddenly made a lunge at me and pushed me out of the way…' Her voice grew jerky and, shuddering, she stopped speaking.

Stephen stretched out a hand and covered hers.

That brief but reassuring touch steadied her and, after a moment she went on, 'All I could see was a dark shape, not even a glimmer of a face. But I'm sure it was a man, and I think he must have had something black over his head.'

'You're right on both counts. As I came in response to your cry, I caught just a glimpse of him slipping out through the French windows.' Shaking his head in frustration, Stephen went on.

'By the time I'd made sure you weren't hurt he'd made his escape. I got the servants up to search the garden.

'Roberto's just reported that there was no sign of any intruder, but they found a torch that had been dropped and broken, and the gate into the *campo* wasn't properly closed. Presumably whoever it was left in too much of a hurry to notice…'

Watching his mouth as he spoke, the slight gleam of his white, even teeth, the way his lips moved, she recalled how those beautiful sensuous lips had coaxed and teased hers… How they had traced the curves of her breasts and closed around an eager nipple… Her stomach clenched at the memory.

To distract herself from these erotic thoughts, she asked a shade raggedly, 'Is there much crime in Venice?'

'Comparatively little, and there's hardly any street crime. Unlike some cities, Venice is a safe place to walk around at night.'

'But I suppose if a gate were accidentally left open and a would-be thief saw an opportunity—'

Stephen shook his head. 'I don't think it's as simple as that. Roberto assured me that when he did his nightly rounds before going to bed, all the gates were securely fastened. So this was more than opportunism. I believe it was premeditated.'

Sophia's eyes widened in shock. 'Premeditated?'

He nodded. 'Our intruder almost certainly came in the same way he went out—through the French windows of your sitting-room.

'As you may have noticed, we have an electronic security system and, as he managed to gain entrance to the garden and the house without setting off any alarms, I'm inclined to think that he had keys to both the gate and the French windows.'

Sophia's voice still trembled. 'Do you think he came in that way presuming the suite would be empty?'

'It's possible. On the other hand, it could have been his target. He might have been looking for something in particular, something he hoped would be there, when he heard you coming.'

After a thoughtful silence, Sophia remarked, 'But if he was looking for something in particular, rather than just being there to steal, why did he bother going through my case?'

'Hard to say.' Then crisply, 'You're quite sure there's nothing missing?'

'The only thing I brought that was of any real value was the jewellery box I had for my birthday, and that's still there, thank heaven…'

She wondered whether to mention her suspicion that someone had searched her flat in London, but after a moment she decided against it. He might only think she was paranoid.

Instead she said, 'I don't understand why whoever it was decided to stay and hide rather than making a run for it.'

'Presumably he was waiting for you to go to sleep so he could sneak out unnoticed. If he'd locked the windows and the gate behind him, no one would have been any the wiser. The only indication that anything was amiss would have been the fact that the lights had been tampered with.'

'How did he manage that?' she asked, her vulnerability making her shudder.

'By the simple expedient of removing the bulbs.'

So, if he hadn't been disturbed, all he would have needed to do was replace the bulbs and no one would have been any the wiser... But what could he have been looking for...?

While Stephen sat quietly watching her, trying to follow her train of thought, he ran lean fingers over his jaw, which was slightly roughened by the beginnings of a golden stubble.

Hearing the faint rasp, she glanced up and, watching the seductive movement, felt an almost overpowering urge to touch him, to trace the outline of his mouth and the fascinating cleft in his chin, then to follow her fingertip with her lips and let them linger there...

'More brandy?'

Huskily she said, 'No, thank you. I'm starting to feel distinctly fuddled now.'

'Then I think it's high time you went to bed. You must be absolutely shattered.' Rising to his feet, he added, 'Just give me a minute or so to replace your light bulbs...'

After a comparatively short time, he returned to say, 'There... All set.'

Her habitual caution, her self-control, her pride, even her common sense, had all been thrown into the melting pot by what had happened, and the last thing she wanted to do was to go back to her own suite and sleep alone.

Strong emotions were said to trigger off and strengthen other emotions and, when her fear had faded, the torment, the longing, the sweet desire, had returned, more powerful than ever.

She wanted to be with him, to lie in his arms, to sleep with him. But, after the way she had treated him earlier, there was no way she could let him know how she felt.

When she pushed aside the blanket and·stood up, as though sensing her unspoken reluctance, he asked, 'Any problems?'

'Not really.' She turned away.

He caught her wrist, holding it lightly but firmly, refusing to let her go. 'Come on, you may as well tell me what's bothering you.'

Shaken to the core by his touch, wanting to tell him, but afraid to in case he was still angry enough to get his revenge by spurning her, she denied, 'It's nothing.'

'Tell me,' he insisted.

Realizing he wasn't going to let her go until she'd told him *something,* head bent, so that the light cast the shadow of her long lashes on to her cheeks, she mumbled, 'Earlier you said that the intruder might have keys… You don't think he'll come back tonight?'

'I very much doubt it but, to be on the safe side, I've a couple of men out there waiting.'

'That's a relief,' she said hollowly.

'Look, if you don't fancy going back to your own suite, and I wouldn't blame you in the slightest if you didn't, you can sleep in my bed.'

Her breath caught in her throat and for a second she was utterly still.

Misinterpreting her reaction, he said with an edge to his voice, 'Don't worry, I wasn't planning to be in it with you. What I meant was, we'll change rooms, if that's what you want?'

Her voice scarcely above a whisper, she said, 'I don't want to sleep alone.'

'Now there you might have a problem. I'm only flesh and blood, and if we share a bed I'm not sure I'll be able to keep my hands off you.'

Made bold by the knowledge that he still wanted her, she said, 'That's just it; I don't want you to.'

There was a moment of utter stillness, then he asked, 'Are you quite sure you mean that?'

'Yes, I'm quite sure.'

'Isn't it a high price to pay to feel safe?'

'I don't want to feel safe.'

She wanted to love and feel loved. But of course he didn't love her. She would have to make do with loving him.

'What's happened to the cautious woman who said it was too soon, we didn't know one another?'

She looked up at him, her big, doe eyes asking him to take her with him to bed. 'Perhaps it's due to the fright I had, but that woman no longer exists.'

With a little laugh of triumph, he swept her into his arms and carried her through to his bedroom.

Setting her down by the handsome four-poster, the duvet of which was turned back ready, he said softly, 'Let me look at you.'

She stood in a pool of golden light spilt by the bedside lamp, tall and gracefully proportioned, with straight shoulders, a slim waist and long legs.

Her ivory satin nightdress, cut on the cross, clung lovingly to her slender figure, focusing his attention on the curve of her hips and the shadowy hollow between her breasts, until the gleaming spaghetti straps drew his eyes up to the smooth creamy skin of her shoulders and throat, and beyond.

Her beautiful almond eyes were glowing and a faint flush of colour lay along her high cheekbones. A tendril of dark silky hair curled against her cheek and, as he studied her, the tip of a pink tongue stole out to moisten her dry lips.

It was unconsciously provocative and, taking her face between his palms, he let his tongue-tip follow where hers had been, before kissing her with an unbridled passion that sent her up in flames.

When she was limp and quivering in his arms, he stripped off her nightdress and laid her on the bed.

Then sitting beside her, he ran his hands over her naked flesh, bringing every nerve-ending in her entire body to life.

Murmuring how beautiful she was, how much he wanted her, he caressed her neck and shoulders and her firm, surprisingly full, breasts, before taking one of the dusky pink nipples into his mouth and suckling sweetly.

Hearing her indrawn breath, he intensified the pleasure by teasing the other nipple with his finger and thumb.

When she began to gasp, he stripped off his short robe and, stretching out beside her, continued the exquisite torment until quivers of delight were running through her.

Then, his free hand stroking down her flat stomach to the triangle of dark silky curls and the smooth warm skin of her inner thighs, he used his long fingers to drag all sensation downwards. Until, like a finely balanced orchestra, a combination of the two produced such exquisite sensations that she began to shudder and make soft, inarticulate sounds deep in her throat.

When he lowered himself into the cradle of her hips, she felt his weight with pleasure. This was her man, her love, the moment of truth she had been waiting for.

Then all thoughts ceased and only feeling remained as, his mouth on hers, he made love to her ardently, skillfully, with a tenderness and passion that brought them to a shattering, and shared, climax.

When the heavens righted themselves and she floated back to earth, his legs entwined with hers, his fair head pillowed on her breast, she had never felt so joyous, so complete and ful- filled and utterly happy.

Now she knew why love inspired poets and musicians, writers and philosophers, why people averred that it made the world go round.

After a while he lifted himself away and kissed her tenderly. Then, switching off the light, he drew her close and settled her head on his shoulder.

She gave a sigh of pure contentment and snuggled against him. At last she was home and—in the country phraseology her father had remembered from his childhood—where she belonged to be.

For the first time since his death, rather than making her sad, the thought of her father added to her warmth and gladness.

He would be pleased for her. Happy that, by some miracle— a miracle she still didn't understand and which, looked at ob- jectively, seemed utterly incredible—she had found the man in his portrait, the man of her dreams.

It was mid-morning when she awoke and sunshine was stream- ing in. She was alone in the bed, but that wasn't surprising. The small oval watch she always wore showed it was almost ten-thirty.

In spite of feeling just a bit guilty, she smiled to herself. A little like the cat who got the cream.

Not once, but twice, during the night, as though he couldn't get enough of her, Stephen had kissed her into wakefulness and they had made love again.

She had thought it couldn't possibly get any better but—as though her body had now fully awakened to feelings it had pre- viously never known—it did.

The first time, when she'd stirred and opened her mouth to his kisses, after satisfying himself that she was fully aroused, he had made love to her hard and fast, without mercy, as though he'd enjoyed hammering home his mastery.

The second time his love-making had been slow and lingering, drawing out the pleasure, making her writhe and gasp and moan with frustration before he drove deeper to give her the satisfaction she craved.

How had she lived all those years without him? Without really knowing what love could be like?

A love that combined the spiritual and physical, that filled her heart and mind and soul, had to be the most wonderful boon that life could bring.

The only gift greater would be the knowledge that he felt the same kind of love for her.

He had told her she was beautiful, had told her how much he wanted her and, while that was a far cry from *loving,* it was a start.

In the meantime, she had a job to do.

Her nightdress had been placed over a chair and, climbing out of bed, she pulled it on and, her heart singing, made her way into the living-room.

Finding no sign of Stephen, she hurried through to her own suite.

Perhaps her sunny mood coloured everything because even the sight of the oriental screen and the memory of that dark, lurking figure, no longer held any terrors for her.

Happiness bubbling inside her like a hidden spring, she showered, cleaned her teeth and put on a light cotton dress and sandals. Then, having decided it was much too hot for make-up, she took her hair up in a dark gleaming coil and went in search of Stephen.

The suite appeared to be deserted except for a young maid

who was vacuuming the living-room carpet. In answer to Sophia's query, the girl told her that, having breakfasted some time ago, Signor Haviland was in his office.

When she went along and tapped at the door, he called, 'Who is it?'

Just the sound of his voice making her go weak at the knees, she answered, 'It's Sophia.'

A second later the door opened and he was there, wearing well-cut casual trousers and a white shirt open at the neck. He looked bright-eyed and fit in spite of his own lack of sleep.

Smiling down at her, he said, 'Good morning, sleepyhead. Or should I say good afternoon?' Then, dropping a light kiss on her lips, he observed, 'You look happy.'

'I am happy,' she said simply.

'No lingering terrors?'

She shook her head.

'Certain?'

'Quite certain.'

In fact she had a great deal to thank the mysterious intruder for, she thought with a touch of irony. If it hadn't been for him, instead of sharing a night of utter bliss that had turned her world into a glorious place, she would have slept alone and been utterly miserable.

And this morning, instead of being warm and close, her relationship with Stephen would no doubt have been distant and chilly.

And that didn't bear thinking about.

'So the therapy worked,' Stephen remarked with a wicked, sidelong grin.

'Therapy? Is that what it was?' Sophia did her best to sound indignant.

'Amongst other things.' He bent and kissed her again, gently at first, then with a growing ardour.

After a moment or two, his lips still clinging closely, he drew her into the office and shut the door. Setting her back to the panels, he ran his hands over her while he deepened the kiss until every bone in her body melted.

When he'd finally freed her lips, he said huskily, 'I've been wanting to make love to you again ever since I first woke.'

Amazed at her own boldness, she said, 'You could have wakened me.'

He kissed the tip of her small straight nose. 'After keeping you awake half the night?'

Watching the colour creep into her cheeks, he added, 'To be honest, I almost did, but in the end I hadn't the heart to disturb you. You looked much too beautiful, all tousled and dewy with sleep…

'It was as much as I could do to tear myself away, but I had some business that wouldn't wait…'

After another lingering kiss, he murmured softly, 'I thought if you were still in bed when my business was completed, I might come back and join you.'

Stifling the feeling of regret and trying to sound stern, she said, 'Then it's just as well I'm up, otherwise the best part of the day would have been—'

He stopped the words with a finger to her lips. 'Don't say *wasted,* or you'll hurt my feelings.'

As she gazed up at him, he traced the outline of her mouth before removing his finger.

Her voice not quite steady, she told him, 'I was going to say, *over before I'd got any work done.*'

'Who cares about work?'

He sounded light-hearted, almost as if he were in love.

It was a heady thought and she was clutching it to her when he said prosaically, 'Would you like me to ring for some fresh breakfast? You must be hungry.'

She shook her head. 'Considering how late it is, and the fact that I had an excellent meal last night, I think I'd prefer to wait for lunch.'

'Fruit juice? Tea? Coffee?'

'Coffee would be nice, if it won't be too much trouble for the staff?'

'No trouble at all. There'll still be hot coffee in the morning room.'

Seeing he was about to accompany her, she objected, 'I don't want to take you away from your work.'

'I've done all that's necessary for the moment. Anything else will keep until I feel like dealing with it. In any case it's too nice to work…'

He led her through to the attractive morning room where, on the sideboard, along with the remains of breakfast, was a hotplate with a glass jug of coffee.

Filling two cups with the fragrant brew, he added a little cream and sugar to hers as he knew she liked it and, leaving his own black and sugarless, came to sit beside her.

As they drank, he asked, 'So where shall we go? All Venice is out there just waiting to be explored.'

Taking a firm grip on her excitement, she said severely, 'I'm supposed to be here to work.'

'If you insist, I'll let you work for an hour or so, then we'll go out… So start deciding what you'd like to see.'

'I don't mind in the slightest,' she told him happily. 'I'll leave it to you.'

'Well, if you do think of anywhere, let me know.'

A shade hesitantly, she said, 'Sooner or later I'd like to see Harry's Bar. I know it's a very touristy thing to want to do, but—'

'Not at all… It's an experience that shouldn't be missed.' Pausing to take a sip of coffee, he went on. 'It first opened in the early nineteen-thirties and some very famous people went there, including Ernest Hemingway and Maria Callas.

'Even today you'll find it isn't just the haunt of tourists. There's nearly always a fascinating mix of people—writers and artists, photographers and film stars, the rich and famous, the notorious and the flamboyant... Why don't you change your mind about working and we'll go now?'

The coaxing smile, the mischievous gleam in his eye, made him almost irresistible.

Sorely tempted, she hesitated. Then her normal self-discipline kicked into action, making her ask, 'But didn't you say the first viewing was in six weeks' time?'

'Yes, I did,' he admitted ruefully.

'Then, before I even consider going out, I ought to have a look at the paintings and get some idea of how much work will be needed to get them ready.'

'A woman with principles, I see.'

'They're no rarer than a man with principles.'

He held up his hands in mock surrender. 'I'm not suggesting they are. I wouldn't dare!'

His voice serious, he added, 'But I haven't met too many of them... As you said yesterday, I must have been associating with the wrong kind of women...'

She laughed ruefully. 'You sound quite bitter.'

'Not at all. A little disillusioned, perhaps...'

She waited, hoping he would go on, but all he said was, 'More coffee?'

'No, thanks. I enjoyed that thoroughly, but I don't need any more.'

'Come along, then. We'll go up to the Long Gallery first and have a quick look at the family portraits.'

They were just leaving the room when Rosa appeared to

clear away the remains of breakfast. '*Buon giorno, signorina*,' she greeted Sophia with a smile.

Smiling back, Sophia said, '*Buon giorno.*'

'Would you like me to bring you some fresh breakfast?' the housekeeper asked.

'No, thank you, Rosa. I've had a cup of coffee and, as it's so late, I've decided to wait until lunch time to eat.'

Turning to Stephen, Rosa queried, 'Will you be home for lunch and dinner, Signor Stefano?'

'I thought we would have dinner here tonight, but we won't be at home for lunch. In a little while I'll be taking the *signorina* out to see some more of Venice.'

Rosa nodded and beamed, before asking, 'Do you like our beautiful city, Signorina Jordan?'

'Indeed I do. In fact it was love at first sight.'

Beaming, Rose said, 'I remember it was just the same when your fa—'

'We'd best be moving,' Stephen broke in with a brusqueness that surprised Sophia. 'Otherwise we'll get nothing done before lunch.'

Leaving Rosa looking disconcerted, he hurried Sophia to the door.

His hand was on the knob when he turned to say more gently, 'By the way, Rosa, will you tell Angelo we'll have dinner at eight…?'

'Of course, Signor Stefano.'

'Oh, and if anything urgent should happen to crop up, we'll be in either the Long Gallery or the old family apartments.'

Closing the door behind them, he put a hand at Sophia's waist and escorted her through to the hall.

As they climbed the stairs she found herself wondering why he had been so curt with Rosa. It wasn't like him at all.

CHAPTER SEVEN

THE Long Gallery was truly spectacular, with a gleaming marble floor and a magnificent ornate ceiling. On its panelled walls hung a series of oil paintings which, Stephen told her, spanned almost six centuries.

'This is one of the most notable.' He indicated a portrait of a stern-faced man with heavy black brows, wearing the traditional trappings of a doge.

'Giovanni Fortuna was doge in the late fourteen-hundreds and, as you can probably tell, this portrait was painted by Gentile Bellini...

'And that—' he pointed to a very distinguished and haughty-looking older woman, wearing an elaborate black gown and a double rope of lustrous pearls '—is Aunt Fran's great-great-grandmother. It was painted by Raphael Anafesto.'

Reminded of the pearls the woman in her father's miniature had been wearing, Sophia remarked, 'The pearls are beautiful.'

Stephen glanced at her before answering, 'Yes, they're the famous Padova Pearls, the ones that Paolo was hoping to get his hands on.'

Before she could ask what had happened to them, Stephen was moving on. 'This is a Foscari...'

As they strolled along the gallery, he told her who had

painted the various portraits, who the sitters were and how they fitted into the family.

'What about that one?' Sophia pointed to a portrait of a strikingly beautiful dark-haired girl wearing a hairstyle and clothes that must have dated from the early nineteen-thirties.

'Ah, in that case the artist is unknown, but the sitter is Lucia Fortuna, a distant cousin who lived at Verona…'

Finally, they came to a portrait of two little girls of perhaps four years old, sitting solemnly side by side and holding hands.

Both with dark hair and dark eyes, they were dressed identically in pink flounced dresses and matching ribbons.

'Twins!' Sophia exclaimed delightedly. 'What are their names?'

'Silvia and Francesca. Silvia, the little girl on the left, is my mother, and the one on the right my Aunt Fran.'

With a hint of sadness, he added, 'They were always extremely close.'

'Is your mother still alive?'

'Very much so. She's still a beautiful woman who looks nothing like her age.'

'There's no other portrait of her here?'

'Unfortunately not. After the twins were painted, no more family portraits were added.'

Gazing at the two dark-haired children, Sophia remarked, 'You're nothing at all like your mother or your aunt.'

'No,' he agreed. 'I take after my father both in looks and temperament.'

'Is he…?'

'He's as fit as a fiddle and, after a lifetime of hard work, enjoying an early retirement. At the moment he and my mother are travelling, seeing the world and enjoying each other's company.

'My mother was a great deal luckier than Aunt Fran. After

more than thirty years of marriage, she and my father are still lovers in the best and truest sense of the word…'

By this time they had reached the end of the gallery, and Stephen asked, 'So what do you think of the family portraits?'

Sophia had found some of them striking, some charming, some not quite so charming, but all of them interesting, and she said so. She adding, 'You weren't planning to part with any of them?'

He slanted her a glance. 'Would you?'

'No, I think it would be a terrible shame—' She broke off abruptly. 'I'm sorry, I shouldn't have said that. It's really none of my business.'

'Well, I *did* ask you… Incidentally, Gina thinks I should get rid of the lot while the art dealers are here in force.'

'Well, of course if you need the money for the Palazzo's upkeep…' Sophia began awkwardly.

'I don't.'

'Then personally I would keep them.' Sophia looked back wistfully at the impressive painting.

Stephen enjoyed the look of wonderment in her eyes. 'Is that because art is your thing?'

'Partly, I suppose,' she answered honestly. 'But mainly because, kept here together, they make a unique and fascinating family tree.'

'You're right, of course. Aunt Fran felt the same. And for that reason alone I've no intention of parting with any of them.

'Now, suppose we go and take a look at the ones that my aunt had decided to sell?'

He led the way along to what had once been the family's apartments before they had been forced to move downstairs.

All the rooms were grand and spacious, apart from a small simply furnished sitting-room-cum-study that Stephen told her had been his aunt's.

'This was her very own private space. It's where she wrote

her diary and dealt with her correspondence, or used as a refuge when she wanted to be alone with her music.

'And next door, in complete contrast, is the main living-room…'

The main living-room was undeniably splendid, but the flowers and photographs, the homely touches that brought the downstairs living-room to life, were missing, leaving it somewhat formal.

Even so, as Sophia gazed at the lofty ceiling with its crystal chandeliers, the long, gilt-framed mirrors on the walls, the handsome marble fireplace and the old leaded windows with their arched tops and small uneven panes of pale, slightly different-coloured glass, she felt a strong affinity for it. As if, rather than the room being strange, she already knew and liked it.

Seeing Stephen was watching her curiously, she said, 'You're quite right about the windows; they're absolutely glorious… In fact, as you said, it's a beautiful room altogether.'

He smiled. 'I'm glad you agree.'

'The odd thing is, I feel as if I've seen it before… I don't mean just as a picture in some magazine, but as if I *know* it, as if I'd once been happy here…'

It was ridiculous of course; she'd never been to Venice and, if she had, she would have been staying at some hotel rather than a grand palazzo.

But, even as she told herself it was just a mistaken impression, an illusion, as though recalling some distant dream, she could picture herself as a small child sitting by those windows on someone's knee.

A woman who had smiled at her and hugged her. A woman who, when they had risen, had taken a sparkling diamond solitaire from her finger and, stooping, had scratched *Sophia* on one of the uneven panes of glass…

'What is it?' Stephen asked. 'You look as if you've gone into a trance.'

His voice shattered the spell, breaking up the image like a stone thrown into water created ripples that brake up the reflections.

Her voice soft and uncertain, she said, 'I'm afraid I was daydreaming.'

'Tell me about it.'

'It was strange, like pictures forming inside my own head...'

'Go on.'

'I was quite young...sitting on a woman's knee... She wrote my name on one of the window panes with a diamond ring...'

'Whereabouts? Which window?'

Without conscious thought, Sophia answered, 'The middle window, about a metre from the ground.'

As she spoke, she walked over to look.

In the corner of one of the panes, at the right height—a young child's height—and just as she'd visualized it, faint and slightly spidery, but quite unmistakable, was the name *Sophia*...

'Well, well, well...' Stephen, who had followed her, murmured softly.

Straightening, she lifted a startled face. 'I don't understand... If I've never been here before—and how *could* I have been?—how does my name come to be there?'

'It may not be your name. Aunt Fran was named Francesca Sophia...'

'Oh...' It was almost a relief.

'But of course that doesn't explain how you knew the name was there.'

As she gazed at him, he added, smiling, 'Unless you're psychic?'

She shook her head. 'Not that I know of.'

'Then it's a mystery...' Running his finger down her cheek, he went on. 'Don't look so worried. Left to their own devices, mysteries have a habit of solving themselves.'

Giving her shoulder a little squeeze, he went on, 'Now, I suggest you take your mind off it by having a preliminary look at the paintings Aunt Fran earmarked to go.'

'Where are they kept?'

'Right here in this room.'

Opposite the fireplace, at about the same height as the mantelpiece, there was a massive, finely carved dark oak cupboard with six sets of double doors that ran from top to bottom.

Walking over to the cupboard, he pointed to a small inconspicuous panel on the wall above. 'This is a special security system that sounds an alarm if anyone tries to open any of the doors without putting in a six letter code word, which in this case is easy to remember.'

He tapped in the word—*Fenice*—before opening the first set of doors.

Sophia saw that the deep space was taken up by a row of pictures that were stored standing edge-on in individual racks.

'Most of these paintings used to be hung in the rooms below,' Stephen explained. 'But when the family moved down to the ground floor, so Aunt Fran could store the paintings up here, she had these special racks fitted.

'This is how they work.' As he spoke, he slid out one of the racks and swivelled it to display the painting, before reversing the process and sliding out the next.

Impressed, she said, 'That's a wonderful system. We could do with something similar at the gallery.'

'It makes them accessible and easy to view…. Incidentally, when you want to move on to the next stage, Aunt Fran had a room fitted out as a workshop, with cleaning materials and everything on hand that you might need.'

'I take it you've looked through the paintings and have some idea of how much work might be involved?' Sophia asked.

Casually leaning up against the rack, he turned to face her.

'To be honest, I haven't seen any of them properly for quite a while, certainly not since they were transferred up here.

'But I believe that most of them are in a reasonable state. If there are any that require a great deal of work they can be left until one of the later viewings.'

'It seems a shame they've been hidden away.'

'Though some of them are undeniably masterpieces they're on the gloomy side. If I remember rightly, the subjects—apart from religion—are mainly death and destruction and gory hunting scenes.

'Hardly the sort of thing you'd want to look at day in, day out—' He laughed.

A knock at the door cut through his words and Rosa came in looking slightly hassled. 'I'm sorry to bother you, Signor Stefano, but the Marquise is here and she insists on speaking to you. She says it's very important.'

He nodded. 'Thank you, Rosa, I'll be right down.'

As the door closed behind the small upright figure, Stephen said with a sigh, 'I'd better go and see what the problem is... If you'd like to carry on, I'll be back as soon as possible.'

At the door, he turned to say, 'Oh, by the way, in the right-hand drawer of Aunt Fran's desk there's a handwritten catalogue of the pictures and what's known about their provenance.'

He blew her a kiss and departed.

Smiling at the romantic gesture, Sophia went through to the small sitting-room.

This was the room Stephen's aunt had used as a refuge when she'd wanted to be alone. Other people had been shut out, kept at bay, and Sophia knew she should have felt like an intruder.

But somehow she didn't. Always sensitive to atmosphere,

she felt welcome, wanted, as she stood for a moment or two looking around her.

On a cream carpet, in front of a pretty tiled fireplace flanked by bookshelves, stood a soft leather couch and a low table.

One wall was taken up by a rosewood piano with gilt sconces on either side to hold candles, while opposite stood a matching writing-desk with drawers at the top, and below—each side of the arched knee space—a cupboard.

The simple, but charming, room said a lot about its previous mistress, and Sophia found herself wishing she had known the woman who had owned Ca' Fortuna.

She sighed, then reminding herself that she had work to do, she crossed to the desk and opened the top drawer. There, along with neat piles of stationery, was the catalogue she was looking for.

It was handwritten in a clear, neat script and a quick glance through showed it to be well-ordered and comprehensive. Sophia smiled to herself, remembering how Stephen had described his aunt as 'businesslike when necessary'.

Taking the catalogue, a piece of clean paper and a borrowed pen, she closed the drawer carefully and, returning to the main living-room, began to look through the paintings, making notes as she went.

Though magnificent in their way, the canvases were, as Stephen had said, gloomy. Ideal for an avid collector or hung in a museum, but not the kind of thing most people would want to see on their walls.

Though one or two would benefit from being cleaned, most of them appeared to be in good condition and on the whole there was much less work involved than she had anticipated.

Which was good news.

Or was it?

Surely that would depend on how Stephen really felt about her.

Though he'd been both tender and passionate, did he think of their relationship as just a physical thing, a short-term affair that would end when her work here was done and she went home?

Common sense told her he probably did.

Hope insisted that he might not. That there might be a spark which, given time, might ignite and grow into a lasting flame.

She tried hard to cling to that thought.

But, either way, now she had committed herself, it was too late for regrets…

The door opening made her look up with a smile—a smile that died on her lips when, instead of Stephen, the Marquise walked in.

Expertly made-up, her black hair smooth and glossy as a raven's wing, her lips a gleaming carmine, she was wearing fine stockings and high heels and an expensive-looking silk two-piece of shimmering purply-blue that showed off her voluptuous figure and made her look strikingly elegant.

In her off-the-peg cotton dress and sandals, with her legs bare and her face innocent of make-up, Sophia felt unattractive and dowdy beside her.

With a smile that failed to reach her eyes, and almost a sneer in the words, the Marquise remarked in her excellent but stilted English, 'I see you are hard at work, Signorina Jordan. I hope you are getting on well?'

'Not particularly,' Sophia answered pleasantly. 'All I've managed to do so far is take a preliminary look through the paintings.'

'That is not surprising, really. Stefano told me how you had made a very late start…'

Surely he hadn't told her *why*?

'A night-time intruder, I understand?'

Sophia breathed a sigh of relief. 'Yes.'

'You must have been very much afraid?'

Sophia looked up at her and replied as confidently as she could. 'At the time, I was.'

'I have no doubt Stefano was soon on the spot to comfort you.'

Sophia said nothing and after a moment the Marquise went on. 'So, having slept late, you have not yet had a chance to estimate how much time it will take to get the paintings ready?'

Unwilling to tell this arrogant woman the truth, Sophia said mendaciously, 'No, I'm afraid not.'

'Yet Stefano tells me that, instead of working, you and he intend to spend the afternoon sightseeing.'

'It was his suggestion.'

The Marquise narrowed her eyes at Sophia's reply. 'Well, I feel that for your own sake you should get on with what you are being paid to do and make your stay in Venice as brief as possible.'

'For my own sake?'

'Venice is not always a healthy place to be.'

'What exactly do you mean by *healthy?*' Sophia asked, her voice even.

The Marquise waved a scarlet-tipped hand. 'Nothing in particular. Just that you might find it…safer in London. There is always an element of…shall we say…*danger* in a city that is not one's own, don't you think?'

It sounded almost like a threat. But, deciding to take it at face value, Sophia said composedly, 'Judging by what I've heard so far, Venice is a very safe city.'

'Of course for most people it is. But I think you would be wise to work quickly, without distractions, and return to London as soon as possible.'

'If you'll excuse me saying so, I don't really see that it's any of your business.' Sophia tried to sound confident but the Marquise's words were worrying her.

The beautiful black eyes flashed fire. 'That is where you are wrong. Anything that affects Stefano *is* my business. He should be getting on with his work, his plans for the future, without having to run around after a *guest*…'

The word was spat out with such venom that Sophia guessed Stephen must have referred to her in precisely that way.

'Surely that's up to him to decide,' she pointed out quietly.

'He is being stupidly…' the Marquise paused, searching for the right adjective, before ending triumphantly '…quixotic. His time is far too precious for him to waste it trailing round Venice with a chit of a girl who has the hots for him.'

When Sophia stayed silent, the Marquise asked contemptuously, 'Have you no comment to make?'

'Only that your choice of words is unbecoming, to say the least. But then if someone is jealous—'

'How dare you speak to me like that? Why should I need to be jealous of a working class little nobody like you? Do not imagine that you pose a threat. Stefano and I have the same social status, the same background…'

Knowing there was quite a lot of truth in the Marquise's words further depleted what small amount of self-confidence Sophia had left.

'And make no mistake about it,' the other woman went on viciously, '*I* am the one he loves, the one he intends to marry…

'Oh, yes, he may be amusing himself with you at the moment. Judging by the glow about you, I dare say he is. But *amusing himself* is all it amounts to.

'Stefano is a very attractive man, and if a cheap little slut chooses to throw herself at him, who can blame him for accepting what is offered?

'But you are wasting your time if you think you have the faintest chance of catching him merely by going to bed with him. Women much more beautiful than you have tried and failed.

'Stefano is mine. He's always been mine. We were intended

to be together. If I had not been foolish enough to—' She broke off abruptly, then repeated, 'Stefano is mine.'

Struggling to hold on to her composure, Sophia asked, 'If he is, as you say, yours, why should he want to take *me* to bed?'

'Because he is a red-blooded man and I am still officially in mourning. But after we are married and I am his wife, his little flings will be over and done with. All in the past. He will remain faithful to me because that is the kind of man he is.

'So you see, Signorina Jordan, you have nothing to keep you in Venice and, as I pointed out a little while ago, it might be dangerous to stay.

'My earnest advice to you is, pack your things and go home now, today, before something unpleasant happens to you—'

A knock at the door, which she had left slightly ajar, cut across the Marquise's words.

'Who is it?' she asked.

The door opened further and Rosa came in.

'What do you want?' the Marquise demanded sharply.

Her face and voice without expression, Rosa said, 'I'm sorry to disturb you, but Signor Longheni is on the phone. He said he was hoping to catch you before you left…'

'Tell him I'll be there in a moment.'

As Rosa vanished to do her bidding, the Marquise looked at Sophia with glittering eyes. 'Don't forget what I've told you.'

She swung on her heel and headed for the door.

Sophia was just breathing a sigh of relief when, her hand on the latch, the Marquise turned to deliver her parting shot. 'If you know what is good for you, you will say nothing of this conversation, simply tell Stefano you are not up to the job and get the next plane home.'

A second later the door closed behind her with a decisive click.

Standing staring after her, badly shaken in spite of her

outward show of composure, Sophia wondered how much, if anything, of what had been said was true.

While she didn't want to believe any of it, she was forced to admit that some of it *might* be.

Her remaining confidence ebbed away.

It *might* be true that Stephen was simply amusing himself. She had been aware of that possibility right from the start.

Even so, her own feelings were so overwhelming that she had been unable to help herself.

But, just because she had been weak enough to sleep with him last night, it didn't mean that she had to sleep with him again.

Surely it would be better to call a halt before she got in any deeper? Hold back at least until she was more certain of just what his motives were?

If he *did* love the Marquise, and she couldn't rule it out, then she didn't want to be involved with another woman's man, didn't want to be *used*…

Yet something told her that if he loved one woman he wouldn't be taking another to bed, and that fitted in with what the Marquise had said about him being faithful after they were married.

After they were married…

The thought was like a knife turning in Sophia's heart. But she had to face it. It *could* be true that Stephen intended to marry his cousin. She was a beautiful woman, they belonged in the same world, and he obviously cared about her.

But if he *was* going to marry the Marquise, why had he brought *her* to Venice against his future wife's wishes and, even more puzzling, why had he made love to her so passionately?

If he could be faithful to the woman he loved *after* they were married, why not before?

Unless still being 'officially in mourning' meant that to avoid losing her reputation the Marquise had to be particularly circumspect and, as she had herself pointed out, Stephen was a red-blooded man.

Sophia sighed. While she *wanted* to think well of the man she loved, she recognized that he was only human, a man of flesh and blood with faults and failings, not some statue on a pedestal.

But if he *was* only using her, how could he have made love to her so tenderly, so caringly…?

Of course, if he *didn't* love the Marquise…

But if he *didn't* love her, surely—after what he'd said about marrying for love—he wouldn't be planning to make her his wife?

Perhaps he wasn't.

It could be just wishful thinking on the Marquise's part, a scenario that *might* come true if she was left with a clear field. Maybe she had made everything up simply to get rid of someone she regarded as a possible rival.

After all, if she posed no threat to the other woman's happiness, why had the Marquise felt it necessary to try and scare her into going?

Sophia's self-confidence began to creep back and her spirits, which had sunk to rock-bottom, revived with a bound.

It would be weak and foolish in the extreme to allow herself to be driven away by the possible inventions—or the half-veiled threats—of a jealous woman.

She was here in Venice with the man she loved, and she was staying until she had finished the job she had come here to do, or until such time as *Stephen* wanted her to go.

But she couldn't believe that time had come quite so soon. Remembering his passion the previous night and his ardour this morning, the way he had backed her against his office door and run his hands over her while he'd kissed her…

She sighed, already longing for the coming night and the delight that lay in store…

The realization brought her up short. While she had been

debating, trying to decide whether or not to share Stephen's bed, her subconscious had already made the decision.

Loving him as she did, she wanted to be with him, wanted to lie next to him and feel his naked flesh against hers, wanted his kisses and caresses, another chance, after a lifetime of waiting, to find paradise in his arms.

And it *had* been paradise, she thought, remembering the magic of his hands and his mouth, the smooth ripple of his muscles beneath her palms, the length of his hair-roughened legs against hers and the driving force of his body that had brought so much shared pleasure…

The click of the latch and the door opening brought her back to the present with a jolt.

Smiling at her, Stephen asked, 'How's it going?'

The remnants of her erotic thoughts clinging like cobwebs, she swallowed and said huskily, 'I've just finished looking through the paintings.'

'I'm sorry to have been such a long time,' he apologized, 'but Gina had some urgent business she needed my help with…'

Then, glancing at the notes that Sophia had made, he queried, 'So what's your verdict?'

Trying to sound brisk and businesslike, she told him, 'One or two could do with cleaning, but most of them seem to be in pretty good condition.'

'So there should be no problem getting the first batch ready in time?'

'None at all.'

She waited to see if he would mention a time frame for the remainder, but he didn't. Instead, he came over and, glancing at the last picture she'd been looking at—a depressing depiction of hell and damnation—asked, 'Is there any that you particularly like and suggest I should keep?'

'Not at first glance,' she answered honestly. 'I think I'm

inclined to agree with you that most of them would be better in a museum.'

'That's something of a relief...' Then, with no change of tone, 'What were you thinking about when I walked in? You looked as if you were miles away.'

Ambushed by the unexpected question, she stammered, 'I-I was...'

Putting a finger beneath her chin, he tilted her face up to his. 'So tell me what you were thinking about, and *don't* say work.'

'I wasn't going to.'

'Well?'

'Well what?'

'Don't prevaricate,' he said severely. 'Tell me what you were thinking about that put that look on your face.'

'What look?' she asked innocently.

Putting a hand at her nape, he bent his head and covered her mouth with his, while his free hand found and caressed the curve of her breast.

When he'd kissed her until every nerve-ending was in meltdown and her knees had turned to jelly, he lifted his head and said triumphantly, 'That look.' As she opened dazed eyes, he turned her around and held her against him, so that they were both facing one of the long gilt-framed mirrors.

She saw a handsome fair-haired man with a slight smile on his lips and the expression of a conqueror, and a woman whose dark head came just to his chin. A woman whose green eyes were slumberous, and whose face was soft and dreamy with love.

Had it been a picture, it could have been entitled, 'By Right of Conquest'.

It was a moment or two before it was borne upon her that his expression was merely that of a triumphant male, while hers gave away only too clearly how she felt about him.

To have her deepest emotions exposed so ruthlessly while

his were evidently uninvolved made her feel uncomfortably naked, vulnerable.

His arms tightening around her, he asked, 'Don't you think you look—?'

'If you ask me, I look half baked,' she broke in abruptly and, hoping against hope that he had read it as straightforward passion rather than love, tried to pull free.

Though he looked at her strangely, he let her go without further comment.

Her legs feeling like rubber, Sophia went back to the paintings and, sliding the last one back into place, closed the heavy oak door. Then, picking up the catalogue and her notes, she said, 'I'll just put these away.'

When she returned, her mask of composure pinned firmly in place, he asked, 'Ready for lunch now? You must be starving.'

'I'm getting pretty hungry.'

'What do you fancy?'

'I've been craving spaghetti Bolognese since I arrived. A true taste of Italy,' she said without hesitation.

He laughed. 'Then I know the perfect place. Giorgio makes the best spaghetti bolognese in Venice. But first we'll have a drink at Harry's Bar... Luckily they're only a stone's throw from each other...

'Now, just before we start, let me show you how to set the security alarm. It's quite simple.'

The alarm set, they made their way to the door.

As they descended the stairs a disturbing thought struck her and she asked, 'Is the Marquise coming, by any chance?'

He gave her a quick appraising glance. 'No, she left a few minutes ago. She's having lunch with Giovanni Longheni, an old flame of hers, who's over from the States. A pleasant, considerate man and now, happily, rich, he rang a short time ago to say he'd been detained and would be half an hour late.'

Picking up the relief Sophia was unable to hide, Stephen said carefully, 'When Gina declared her intention of popping up to say hello to you, I wondered if she intended to make herself unpleasant.'

Sophia said nothing and after a moment he pressed, 'So just how unpleasant was she?'

'Not at all,' she lied valiantly.

'I bet!'

She braced herself for more probing questions but, to her relief, he let the subject drop.

CHAPTER EIGHT

WHEN they reached the downstairs hall Sophia asked, 'Do you mind if I stop to pick up my bag?'

'Of course not… By the way, though there's a breeze today, it's even hotter than it was yesterday and the sun's positively blazing down. So may I suggest that you put on some sunscreen and bring a pair of sunglasses, if you have them?'

'Yes, I've brought both.'

He chucked her under the chin, commenting, 'Sensible as well as beautiful.'

When she returned, well coated in sunscreen, her sunglasses in her bag, he was waiting for her in the living-room, his Polaroids tucked into the top pocket of his shirt.

'Do you feel up to walking in this heat,' he asked, 'or shall we take the motorboat?'

'The heat doesn't bother me at all, and I'm wearing flat-heeled sandals, so if we're really going to explore, let's walk.'

Draping his arm across her shoulder's he mused, 'Excellent woman!'

She gave him a little smile 'Don't tell me… Most of the women you know don't like to walk?'

'Sassy, eh? But, as a matter of fact, you're right. Gina won't walk a step that isn't absolutely necessary, unless it involves shopping.'

The mention of the Marquise cast a shadow and, wishing she had resisted the urge to tease him, Sophia fell silent as they left the hall and—their footsteps echoing on the marble floor—took the arched passageway that led to the south entrance.

Outside, it was baking. Even the breeze was hot and the sun was so bright that she was only too glad to put on her sunglasses.

Crossing the same bridge they had crossed the previous evening, they headed through a maze of narrow *calles* and dusty *campos* towards San Marco.

It was one of the quieter parts of the city and, though an occasional television could be heard behind closed shutters, and now and again through an open door they glimpsed a craftsman at work, the streets were deserted.

When Sophia remarked on this, Stephen told her, 'In this kind of heat most Venetians stay indoors, or else in their own shady courtyards...'

But as they reached the busier tourist areas Sophia found that Venice was *en fête*. Crowds thronged the narrow streets and *fondamentas*, sunlight danced and sparkled on the canals, a variety of craft went past like a parade, and flags and pennants waved in the breeze.

People sat beneath gaily striped umbrellas sipping iced drinks and eating, pigeons strutted and cooed and a variety of cats sunned themselves on balconies and window ledges.

'Where exactly is Harry's Bar?' Sophia asked as they approached San Marco.

'Just a few minutes' walk away. It's quite close to the waterfront.'

When the Grand Canal widened out and became the Canale di San Marco, Stephen stopped and, pointing across the blue water, said, 'The strip of land across there is the Giudecca.

'The famous Hotel Cipriani is on the eastern tip. It's surrounded by lush gardens and it's the only hotel in Venice with a swimming pool…

'And this is Harry's Bar…'

Standing on a corner, it looked quiet and discreet, with none of the overt glitz and glamour that Sophia had half expected, and inside, rather than the heavy red plush and gilt she had envisaged, the bar was light and elegant, with a telling simplicity.

As though to confirm Stephen's words, while they both sipped an excellent dry Martini, several very well-known faces came in and went through to the dining-room to have lunch.

'If you prefer it, we can eat here,' Stephen suggested quietly.

She shook her head. 'I'm quite happy to stick with the original plan.'

'Very well, we can lunch here another time.'

'I wonder if Dad ever came here.' Sophia spoke the thought aloud.

'It's quite possible. I noticed some very nice pictures of Venice in his exhibition, so presumably he knew the city well.'

Sophia nodded. 'Very well, I gather.'

'And he liked it?'

'Yes, he loved it.'

He took her hand in his. 'It seems strange that he never brought you.'

'He always said we'd go one day, but though we went abroad while he could still travel, somehow we never got here. Whenever we discussed holiday plans and I suggested Venice, he said, "Perhaps next time".'

'You mentioned that your mother was born in Mestre…' He paused. 'Tell me about her. What was she like?'

'I'm afraid I don't remember much about her. I was barely seven when she died, and all I really know is what Dad told me.' She looked up at him unsure whether to continue, but when he nodded, she told him everything she knew.

'Her name was Maria. She was petite, with dark hair and eyes. Dad described her as being, "As pretty and as delicate-looking as Shelley China". She was an only child, presumably because both her parents were middle-aged before she was born.

'When she was young she suffered from recurring bouts of rheumatic fever, which seriously undermined her health so that she was never very strong.' Sophia toyed with the fabric of her skirt.

Stephen reached out and lifted her chin so that her eyes met his. 'Where did she and your father meet?'

'They first met in Rome, when Dad was with the Diplomatic Service. Her father—my grandfather—was an industrialist, and when he retired, he bought an apartment near the Villa Borghese and moved there with his wife and daughter.

'Dad got to know the family when she and her parents attended one of the social functions at the British Embassy.

'Though she did her best to settle in Rome, apparently she missed Venice and her friends very much so, after she and Dad got engaged, they went back at every opportunity.'

She paused and took a sip of her drink. Then said thoughtfully, 'I've often wondered how she coped after they were married and Dad was seconded to different embassies, whether she still regarded Venice as her home…'

'Well, if the old saying is true, "home is where the heart is"…'

Sophia smiled. 'Yes, you're right. I believe she loved Dad enough to make the moves worth it…'

When their drinks were finished, they said goodbye to Harry's Bar and made their way to Giorgio's. There, sitting in a little *campo* beneath a gaily striped umbrella, they ate the most delicious spaghetti bolognese Sophia had ever tasted and shared a carafe of rich red Chianti.

Though that strong sexual attraction still sparked between them, they were able to talk together easily, like old friends and, her earlier tension forgotten, Sophia was blissfully happy, more than content just to be with him.

Agreeing that Giorgio's coffee was some of the best they had ever tasted, they were both on their second cup when a couple with two young boys came to sit at an adjacent table.

While the newcomers waited for their drinks, the father and the boys, plainly identical twins, began to play some kind of word game.

The children's clear treble voices drew Sophia's attention and, as she began to listen, it soon became evident that the boys, who often answered in unison, were perfectly in tune with each other.

Smiling a little, she remarked on this to Stephen.

He nodded. 'Yes, one twin often seems to know what the other one's thinking.'

'Were your mother and your aunt like that? You said they were very close.'

'Yes, they were, but they hadn't the mental affinity that real twins often share.'

'Oh… I thought they *were* twins. They looked very much alike, and about the same age.'

'There was just twelve hours between them.'

Smiling at her puzzled expression, he went on, 'Though they were successfully passed off as twins, they weren't even sisters…

'Do you remember the portrait of a distant cousin, Lucia Fortuna, that hangs in the Long Gallery…?'

'Yes, a very beautiful girl.'

'That girl was my grandmother. She almost brought disgrace on herself and the family by becoming pregnant when she was just sixteen.

'Margherita and Enrico Fortuna, the couple I've always regarded as my grandparents, were expecting their first child and, because of various problems, they'd been warned that it would almost certainly be their last.

'As Lucia and Margherita were expecting their babies at approximately the same time, Margherita agreed to take Lucia's baby and pass it off as her own child.

'Between them, the two branches of the family managed to hush the whole thing up. Lucia came to stay at the Palazzo "on an extended visit to her relatives" and, after the birth, returned to Verona with her reputation unsullied. While, as far as the rest of the world knew, Margherita had given birth to twins, which she named Silvia and Francesca.'

'What happened to your real grandmother?'

'The deception was so successful that three years later she married the Duke of Radenza…'

'How fascinating,' Sophia breathed.

'It wasn't until after my "grandparents" had died that my mother told me the whole story and I discovered that, though we both have Fortuna blood, the woman I've always called Aunt Fran wasn't my aunt at all…'

Almost to himself, he added, 'Which perhaps in the circumstances is fortunate…'

Before Sophia could ask what he meant, he queried, 'About ready to move?'

'I'm ready when you are. Where shall we go first?'

'If you're agreeable, I suggest we start by taking a look at the Doge's Palace and the Bridge of Sighs, then we can go further afield, perhaps to the Arsenale and Biennale…'

For the remainder of the afternoon, thoroughly enjoying the sunshine and each other's company, they explored Venice.

By the time they had made their way back to the Piazza San Marco and sipped a cocktail at the eighteenth century Gran

Caffè Quadri, it was almost seven o'clock before they started back to the Palazzo to get ready for dinner.

When Sophia would have gone through to the guest suite, Stephen stopped her. 'I gave orders to have your things moved into the bedroom adjoining mine.'

'Oh…' Flushing slightly, she wondered what the house-keeper would think.

Once again he showed that unnerving ability to walk in and out of her mind. 'After what happened last night, Rosa thought it was eminently sensible. Of course, if you have any objections…?'

Though she was well aware that she *ought* to have, that he *ought* to have consulted her first, Sophia silently shook her head.

'I'm sure you'll like it,' he went on. 'It used to be Aunt Fran's bedroom.'

'Is that where she died?'

He gave a quick nod. 'Yes. Does that put you off?'

'No, so long as it doesn't have bad vibes.' Sophia smiled up at him.

'I can assure you that it doesn't. Quite the opposite, in fact. Rosa was very attached to her mistress and, apart from removing her clothes and personal belongings, she's left the room almost exactly as it was. So it has a really nice atmosphere, very reminiscent of a lovely lady.'

'Then I don't have a problem.'

He reached and tucked a stray tendril behind her ear. 'How very sensible! Some women would throw a fit at the bare idea.'

'I suppose it depends on how one looks at things. In a really old place like this it must be almost impossible to sleep in a room where no one has died.'

A gleam in his eye, he said, 'To be honest, I wasn't intend-ing you to sleep there.' Putting a hand beneath her chin, he lifted her face to his. 'I was expecting you to share my bed.'

His calm assumption that she was his for the taking ought

to have riled her enough to arouse her resistance. But just the thought of spending the night in his arms sent her into a spin.

As she gazed up at him, he smiled into her eyes and bent his head to kiss her.

Her lips parted in eager anticipation.

But, before his mouth touched hers, he straightened, and said with a sigh, 'If I give way to the temptation to kiss you now we'll never get in to dinner and, knowing Angelo, I've no doubt he's planned something special.'

On legs that felt somewhat like a rag doll's, Sophia followed Stephen through to what had been his aunt's bedroom.

Glowing with well-polished antiques, it had two long arched windows, a handsome four-poster and a stone fire-place filled with flowers. As he'd said, it was a charming room, comfortable and homely, with a warm and pleasant atmosphere.

Opening a door to the left, he told her, 'This is the door into my room.'

Then indicating two identical doors on the opposite wall, 'Over there is the bathroom and, next to it, Aunt Fran's private dressing-room-cum-sitting-room.'

As Sophia glanced around, she saw that her case had been unpacked and her things put away. The sight of her jewellery box standing on a chest of drawers, looking as if it belonged there, dispersed any last faint traces of doubt.

Watching her face, he queried, 'All right?'

'Quite all right.'

'Then I'll leave you to get ready… I would suggest we shared a shower, but…' Letting the sentence tail off, he went through the communicating door into his own bedroom.

Shivers running up and down her spine at the thought of sharing a shower with him, she laid out a change of clothing and a pair of high-heeled sandals and headed for the bathroom.

She opened the first door and, finding herself in the dressing-room, closed it again.

The second door led into a sumptuous peach-tiled and white-carpeted bathroom, with a sunken bath and a luxurious shower stall.

Some fifteen minutes later, showered and perfumed, wearing a simple silk sheath of midnight-blue and small gold hoops in her ears, her hair taken into an elegant chignon, she returned to the living-room.

Stephen was already waiting for her, freshly shaven and dressed in well-cut evening clothes and a black bow-tie. He looked so attractive, so devastatingly masculine, that every feminine instinct in her responded.

He came over and, taking her hand, looked her over from head to toe.

The simple dress clung to, and emphasized, her slender figure and the chignon drew attention to her neat ears, the pure curve of her cheeks and jaw, her long neck and smooth shoulders.

An afternoon spent in the sun had given her skin a glow, and love had made her green-gold eyes shine and her mouth look soft and inviting.

Lifting her hand to his lips, he said huskily, 'You look like every man's dream come to life.'

Feeling her heart swell, she thought, if she was *his* dream, she was more than contented.

Rather than releasing her hand, he tucked it through his arm and, leading the way to the elegant oak-panelled dining room, seated her at a candlelit table that would easily have seated twelve.

It was beautifully set with fine linen, crystal glasses, fresh flowers and silver candelabra.

Sophia couldn't help wondering if the housekeeper went to all this trouble when Stephen was on his own.

As he opened and poured the wine, her eyes lingering on the

low centrepiece of yellow roses and sweet-smelling stephanotis, she remarked, 'The flowers are really lovely…'

'Rosa's in her element with you here. When I'm alone I often eat in the breakfast room, and she doesn't get much chance to show off her household skills.' Wryly, he added, 'I'm afraid I'm a sad disappointment to her…'

Sophia smiled.

Candlelight reflected in his black pupils, he said softly, 'You're even more beautiful when you smile. It lights up your whole face…'

He stopped speaking as the housekeeper came in with the first course.

'Ah, Rosa, the *signorina* was just saying how lovely the flowers were.'

Rosa looked gratified. 'The Mistress always liked flowers on the table… And this zucchini al basilico soup was one of her favourites.'

Sophia tried a spoonful and was able to say in all honesty, 'It's absolutely delicious.'

Beaming, Rosa said, 'I'll tell Angelo how much you like it…'

The meal, which included finocchio alla toscana, spinach and ricotta gnocchi, pollo alla valdostana and mascarpone and date tart, was wonderful and, apart from a little desultory conversation, they gave it their full attention.

On the surface.

Beneath the surface the sexual tension was gradually building. All Sophia could think about was the coming night and, though her companion appeared to be easy and relaxed, whenever he looked at her, she saw a little lick of flame in his dark grey eyes. When Rosa brought in the cheese and biscuits, Stephen thanked her and asked her to convey their compliments to Angelo.

She smiled and nodded, before asking, 'Would you like your coffee served here or in the living-room?'

After an enquiring glance at Sophia, Stephen answered, 'In the living-room, please, Rosa.'

By the time they returned to the living-room, the house-keeper was just bringing in the tray. As she set it down on the low table, Stephen said, 'Thank you, Rosa. We'll pour our own.'

'Will there be anything else, Signor Stefano?'

'No, nothing else tonight. *Buona notte.*'

'*Buona notte.*'

Eager for the pleasure that awaited them, Sophia would willingly have skipped the coffee but, with a little secret smile, Stephen murmured in her ear, 'We'd better be all sedate and proper and drink our coffee before we have an early night.'

Settling her on the couch, he filled two of the pretty porcelain cups and asked, 'Would you like anything with it? A Tia Maria, perhaps?'

She shook her head.

He poured himself a small brandy and came to sit beside her. As he settled himself his thigh brushed hers, heightening the sexual tension still further.

Trying not to give herself away totally, she looked anywhere but at him.

A small silver-framed snapshot standing on a nearby bookcase caught her eye. Though it was slightly blurred, she could make out Rosa standing rather self-consciously while, seated in reclining chairs, a slimly-built woman with greying hair and a handsome fair-haired man smiled at the camera.

Though the woman's face was curiously familiar, Sophia couldn't place it, but she immediately recognized the man as a much younger Stephen.

'How old were you when that was taken?' she asked.

Following the direction of her gaze, he answered, 'About eighteen, if I remember rightly. We were in the garden and Rosa had just brought out a tray of tea. Aunt Fran had given Roberto a camera for his birthday, and she suggested that he might snap the three of us…

'As you can see it's not a particularly good photograph, but Aunt Fran always liked it. After so many years, she and Rosa were quite close.'

Thoughtfully, he added, 'Rosa misses having a woman around the place. Now that I'm settled in Venice and able to run Haviland Holdings without working all hours, she's hoping I'll get married…'

Remembering the Marquise, Sophia said quickly, 'But you don't intend to?' Then, regretting the question, she stammered, 'W-what I mean is, you haven't been tempted to so far?'

'Oh, I've been tempted, but that was a long time ago. Twice, when I was in my early twenties and still wet behind the ears, I thought I might have found what I was looking for.

'Both women were beautiful, but beauty alone isn't enough. I wanted someone with warmth and depth and integrity, but Roz turned out to be cold and shallow, incapable of being frank or honest.

'Helen, on the other hand, was complex and passionate but—I discovered just in time—totally unprincipled. She swore she loved me, while in reality she was intending to marry me for my money and use it to prop up the man she really loved.' His expression changed as he talked of these women, is eyes became dark, guarded.

'I decided to give marriage a miss for a while. Though I didn't live like a monk, I avoided any serious relationships and concentrated on work.' He smiled, easing the tension.

'After almost a decade, I'm pleased to say it's paid off financially. Haviland Holdings has more than doubled in size and is worth three times as much as it was when I took control.' He leaned back in his chair relaxed and confident.

'Now I think the time's come for a change of lifestyle. At this stage I can relegate work to second place and be with my wife and family as much as I want. With unlimited time at our disposal, we'll be free to enjoy all the pleasures life offers.'

Sophia was pleased he was talking so openly to her. 'Then you do intend to marry and have children?'

'Oh, yes.'

'Because you *want* to, or just out of a sense of duty?' The thought was spoken aloud before she could prevent it.

'You mean, just so I can produce an heir to the family fortune?'

Aware of the hint of steel behind the cool question, she began unhappily, 'I'm sorry, I shouldn't have…'

As the words tailed off, he picked up her hand and gave it a comforting squeeze. 'Taking into consideration what I said in the garden last tonight about filial duty, it was a reasonable assumption.

'But it happens to be the wrong one.

'When I marry it will be because I *want* to, not merely from a sense of duty.'

'I see…' Then, goaded into it by the fear that the Marquise might have been speaking the truth, she asked, 'Have you someone special in mind?'

'Yes, and I'm hoping to make her my wife before too long. I'm turned thirty now and I want, if possible, to have a family while we're both still young.'

Like someone waiting for the guillotine blade to fall, Sophia waited for him to name his future bride, but he said no more.

Though who else could it be but the Marquise?

Maybe *he* was the man who had been in love with her all those years ago?

Sophia felt empty, hollow inside.

The facts, as far as she knew them, seemed to fit. Straight out of university, he would have been young and untried, with little money of his own... And perhaps, for obvious reasons, his family wouldn't have been too keen on the match...

But now he was a mature man in charge of his own life and with no one to answer to. A wealthy man with looks and charisma. A man the Marquise, who was now free to marry again and in need of a rich husband, had no doubt set her sights on. That would account for her possessiveness and unbridled jealousy.

Her throat feeling as though it were full of shards of hot glass, Sophia swallowed.

It would have been bad enough if he'd just been having an *affair* with the Marquise. But the knowledge that he was intending to get married signalled an end to any hopes and dreams she might have been harbouring, and brought such pain that she almost moaned aloud...

'What's wrong?' Stephen asked, noticing she'd grown pale beneath her newly acquired tan. 'You suddenly look shattered.'

'I'm just tired,' she lied.

'Well, that's understandable. We were walking for hours, and you can't be used to heat like that.'

'It's been such a long, cold spring and we've scarcely seen the sun... I'd started to think summer would never come—' Realizing she was babbling, she broke off abruptly.

He rose and, taking both her hands, pulled her to her feet. 'Let's go to bed.'

That lick of flame was back in his eyes.

Pulling her hands free, she said jerkily, 'I don't want to go to bed with you.'

'Don't worry—' his voice was gentle '—if you're too tired to make love, you can just sleep in my arms.'

'I don't want to sleep in your arms... I don't want to share your bed... I don't want to be *used*...'

Through her own pain and turmoil she was aware that he looked as if she'd struck him.

Just at that moment a knock at the door made them both freeze.

'Yes, what is it?' he asked curtly.

The door opened and a flustered-looking Rosa came in. 'I'm sorry to trouble you, Signor Stefano, but Roberto is anxious to have a word with you.'

'Can't it wait until tomorrow?'

She gave him a significant glance. 'I think you should come now.'

'Very well, I'll be there directly.'

Rosa gave a little nod and hurried away.

Stephen sighed and, taking Sophia's face between his palms, dropped a kiss on her lips. 'I don't know what's bothering you, my love, but we'll sort it out when I get back.'

A searching look and another quick kiss, and he was gone, striding after the housekeeper.

Filled with panic and a kind of futile anger, Sophia stood like a statue, staring at the closed door. How could she go to bed with him, knowing that he belonged to another woman?

How could he ask her to?

But, in all fairness, she had been willing enough the previous night, and clearly it was just fun as far as he was concerned.

All he was doing was 'amusing himself', using her to satisfy a need that at the moment it wouldn't be prudent for the Marquise to satisfy.

A more worldly, sophisticated woman might well regard it simply as an exchange of pleasure, a kind of quid pro quo, and think herself lucky that he was such a skilled and generous lover.

But *she* couldn't.

He had called her 'my love' but he *didn't* love her—he would never love her—to him it was just a game, and, because her deepest emotions were involved, she couldn't join in that game.

Perhaps, if it had been just a strong sexual attraction she felt for him, she might have done. But then, had it been merely attraction, if she hadn't *loved* him, she would never have gone to bed with him in the first place.

But *he* didn't know that.

So what was she to do?

Somewhere near at hand a door opened and closed.

She felt a rush of pure panic. He might be back at any minute.

What could she say to him?

How could she face him?

And if she weakened and slept with him after all, knowing he didn't care a jot about her, how could she ever live with herself?

The pleasant room seemed suddenly stifling, suffocating. Blood drumming in her ears, her head feeling as if it were about to burst, her breath coming in shallow gasps, she glanced around her in increasing desperation.

She needed air… Needed to get out of the house… Needed a chance to be alone and think…

Seeing the garden as a sanctuary, she headed blindly for the French windows. Her hand was on the latch when, in the gathering blue dusk, she noticed a movement, a figure.

Someone was out there.

Turning back, she crossed the room and, opening the door into the hall, peered out. To her utmost relief, there was no one in sight.

Her heels clicking on the marble floor, terrified she might meet someone, she fled to the Palazzo's south entrance and after a brief struggle with the latch, pulled open the heavy studded door and let herself out on to the deserted *fondamenta*.

Her only clear idea to escape, to get away, she crossed the bridge and began to walk quickly in roughly the same direction they had taken previously.

A quiet part of the city, with small *campos* and a maze of narrow streets and alleyways, there were very few people about and dusk was closing in rapidly.

But, heedless of her surroundings, her mind a seething mass

of incoherent thoughts and feelings, she hurried on until sheer fatigue forced her to lessen her speed.

Then, at a more moderate pace, she walked until her agitation began to die down and the air, appreciably cooler than it had been earlier, cleared her head enough to enable her to think more lucidly.

So far as she could see, as she didn't intend to sleep with him there were only three options.

She could move back into the guest suite.

Insist on finding some hotel accommodation.

Or return to London as soon as she was able to get a flight.

But either of the first two would mean continuing to work for him and she knew now she couldn't do that. She needed to make a clean break and save herself the pain and anguish of having to see him every day.

So she would take the third option, and go.

Once she had made the decision, she felt a weight lift. All she had to do now was nerve herself to go back and tell him.

But, having left the Palazzo, she didn't *want* to go back and she dreaded the thought of having to see him again.

If she could find a hotel for the night, in the morning she could contact Rosa and ask for her things to be sent over. Then she could get to the airport, either by bus or taxi, and wait for a flight.

If she could find a hotel…

Common sense pointed out that it was already getting quite late and, with the city full of tourists, finding anywhere to stay the night might be easier said than done…

But she couldn't believe that with so many hotels in Venice, there wasn't *one* with a vacancy. It was just a case of finding it.

Leaving without doing the job she had come here to do would be letting Stephen down, but there were enough paintings in reasonable condition for him to be able to hold the first viewing.

And, if he moved quickly enough he could get someone else

to do the valuations and get the remaining pictures ready for the subsequent viewings…

Sophia was still deep in thought when a cat slunk out of the shadows, the moving shape making her jump and focusing her attention.

She became aware that it was quite dark now and everywhere was completely silent and deserted. Surrounded by high walls and closed shutters, she could have been the only person still left alive in the city.

What few lights there were were widely spaced and placed high up on wall brackets, so that between the pools of illumination were long shadowy stretches.

At the end of one alleyway, only a faint gleam of light reflected in the black water prevented her from walking straight into a canal.

Unnerved by the near accident, she decided to head for the tourist areas where there would still be people and lights and perhaps a café where she could sit and have a coffee while she decided how best to go about finding a hotel.

But what use would a café be? She went cold all over as she realized that in her abject panic she had come out without her bag. With no money, credit card or identification she couldn't book into a hotel, even if she could find one.

She would *have* to go back to the Palazzo.

Her heart like lead, she turned to retrace her steps, but she had walked blindly, unheedingly, and after a while she was forced to admit that she was totally lost.

CHAPTER NINE

WHENEVER Sophia caught sight of a street sign she stopped and tried to decipher what it said, but they were set well above head height and, in the badly lit back alleyways, it was impossible to read them.

There, at the end of the *calle,* was another.

As she craned her neck upwards, on the periphery of her vision she saw a furtive movement.

A shiver ran down her spine and the fine hairs on the back of her neck rose as, standing frozen to the spot, she peered into the darkness.

Everywhere was still and silent.

She had just decided that she must have imagined it, when she suddenly recalled what the Marquise had said about Venice being dangerous.

Gritting her teeth to hold back the fear, and telling herself firmly that she mustn't allow the other woman's veiled threats to worry her, she forced herself to walk on.

But now she was jumpy, on edge, and, though she could hear no footsteps other than her own and frequent glances over her shoulder revealed nothing, some sixth sense insisted that she was being stealthily followed.

Avoiding the narrower alleyways and taking the better lit

calles, on legs that felt curiously stiff and alien, she headed in what she fervently hoped was the right general direction for the Grand Canal.

After what seemed an age, but in reality could only have been minutes, she emerged on to a wider street that looked familiar. Surely this was the way to the bridge that crossed the Rio Castagnio?

If it was, she couldn't be very far from the Palazzo. She breathed a sigh of relief. The place she had been so desperate to get away from suddenly spelt security, refuge.

Yes, there was the bridge and, away to the right, was the Grand Canal, the lights of the far bank gleaming on its dark water.

But those lights failed to penetrate the gloom of the Rio Castagnio and the only source of illumination on this stretch of the canal—apart from one or two dim lamps in the little *campo* opposite—was the light from the Palazzo's boathouse and a lantern above the south entrance.

Safety in sight, Sophia hurried towards the bridge and was about to cross when there was a sudden flurry behind her and a violent push sent her hurtling sideways and into the canal.

She screamed once, just before the water—which was surprisingly cold—closed over her head.

As she fought her way to the surface, panicky thoughts raced through her mind.

In the darkness, would she be able to find the steps to enable her to climb out? And, if she *was* able to find them, would her assailant have crossed the bridge and be waiting for her?

Her only other option was to try to swim to the Palazzo's boathouse. But she was a very poor swimmer at the best of times and now, hampered by clothes, she was having a struggle just to keep afloat.

But she must try to stay calm…

The wash from some boat on the Grand Canal came surging

down the Rio Castagnio and smacked into her face, making her cough and splutter. Her head went under and salty water filled her mouth and nostrils.

As she floundered helplessly, gasping and choking, there was a sudden blur of movement and a splash as someone dived in. After a second or two strong arms closed around her.

Filled with blind panic, convinced that whoever it was was trying to drown her, she struggled wildly to free herself.

'Sophia… Sophia…' Stephen's voice urgently repeating her name brought her to her senses.

As she went limp in his arms, he turned on his back and kicked out strongly for the bank.

A few seconds later, while Stephen supported her, another man whom, in the light from a powerful torch, she recognized as Roberto, stretched out willing hands and helped her on to the steps.

She had just found her footing, unsteady on the high heels, when Stephen hauled himself out and stood dripping by her side, fully dressed apart from his jacket and shoes.

'Thank you,' she whispered.

'Are you all right?' he asked urgently.

Through chattering teeth, she managed, 'Yes, quite all right.'

Reaching for his jacket, which he'd tossed on top of his shoes, he put it around her shoulders. Then, turning to Roberto, he said crisply, 'The south entrance has been locked and bolted and I don't want to have to disturb the women, so will you call the boat and ask Carlo to pick us up here? It'll be much quicker than walking through the garden.'

Using a small walkie-talkie which, along with the torch, was attached to his belt, Roberto did as he was asked.

A voice responded, 'I'm very pleased the *signorina* is safe. I'll be with you in less than a minute. I was just on my way back, so luckily I'm quite close.' As he finished speaking they heard the motorboat's engine and saw the beams of its twin lights coming down the Rio Castagnio towards them.

In no time at all it was by the steps and Sophia was being helped into it.

As Stephen jumped lightly in beside her, Roberto picked up the shoes and said, 'I'll take these with me and let the rest of the men know they can call off the search.'

'Many thanks for all your help, Roberto. I'll see you in the morning. *Buona notte*.'

'*Buona notte*, Signor Stefano.'

When they had covered the few hundred yards to the boat-house, Stephen got out and helped Sophia on to the stone landing stage.

Turning to the dark-haired man who was tying up the boat, he said, 'Thanks for your help, Marco. If you'll bolt the door behind you?'

'Of course, Signor Haviland,' the young man said respect-fully. '*Buona notte*.'

'*Buona notte*, Marco.'

Both of them still dripping water, Stephen hurried Sophia across the servants' hall—her high heels clicking, his feet silent—through the family living-room and into his bathroom, where he turned on the shower.

Delayed shock had set in and she was icy-cold and shaking, her brain thrown out of gear, incapable of coherent thought.

When he removed her sandals and started to strip off her saturated clothes, she tried weakly to push him away. 'Leave me alone... I can manage...'

'Don't be a fool,' he said curtly. 'You're in no fit state to manage alone and, if it's your modesty you're worrying about, I've seen you naked before.'

When her last garment had been tossed on to a wet pile, he pulled off his own clothes and, before she could make any further attempt at protest, he half lifted her into the shower and got in beside her.

Her legs threatening to give way beneath her, she clutched at him and he held her as the hot water cascaded over them.

The heat was comforting, therapeutic, and when, after a while, the worst of the shaking stopped, he let go of her and began to remove the pins that held the remains of her chignon.

As the long wet strands fell around her shoulders, he reached for the bottle and shampooed her hair, before doing his own.

Suds ran down their slick bodies and steam rose around them in scented clouds. It was curiously soothing, almost mesmerizing.

By the time he turned off the water and wrapped a bathsheet around her, she was nearly in a trance and stood like a child to be ministered to.

As soon as they were both dry, he produced two towelling robes and belted one around her slender waist before pulling on his own.

Then, having finished drying and brushing her hair, he led her into the living-room and, steering her to a chair, said briskly, 'As it's late and you must be shattered, I suggest we talk in the morning. But, before we go to bed, we could both use a brandy.' Still feeling odd and quivery inside, slightly nauseous, she objected, 'I really don't think I could drink a brandy.'

Ignoring her protest, he went to the sideboard and returned with two glasses of amber liquid.

Noting the determined gleam in his eye, she accepted one without further argument.

Sitting down opposite, he watched approvingly as she lifted it to her lips.

As, shuddering from time to time, she slowly sipped, the strong spirit settled her stomach and completed the job the hot shower and the cosseting had begun.

Remembering that shower, his hands holding her, his naked body brushing against her own, she shivered.

Hoping he hadn't noticed that betraying movement, she glanced at him surreptitiously.

Head bent, he appeared to be miles away.

Such complete abstraction gave her a chance to drink in the sight of him, which she did with all the eagerness of someone dying of thirst—of someone who, only a short time before, had been planning never to see him again.

While she had been in shock he'd been merely her saviour, a source of strength, a comforting presence, kind hands… But now she saw him as a man again, an almost irresistible man who drew her like a magnet.

His absolute stillness lent his posture an air of tenseness and, with a queer pang, she noticed how his long blond-tipped lashes appeared to brush against his hard cheeks.

She longed to touch those cheeks with her fingertips, to trace his mouth and the grooves beside it, to explore that fascinating cleft in his chin—longed to bury her face against the tanned column of his throat and touch the tender hollow at the base of it with her tongue.

She became achingly aware of his long bare legs and the outline of his muscular thighs beneath the terry towelling… She remembered with toe-curling clarity the slight roughness of those thighs against hers—a roughness that had caused a tingle like an electric shock—and the driving force of his body that had brought such delight…

Reining in her erotic thoughts, she tore her gaze away and reminded herself sharply that he'd only been playing with her, that he belonged to another woman. Though every fibre of her being insisted that he should be *hers*, fate had decreed otherwise.

When her glass was empty, in control once more and

anxious to leave temptation behind her, she rose a shade unsteadily to her feet.

His manner mild, his voice pleasant, he queried, 'Were you thinking of going somewhere?'

'You said a brandy and then bed,' she reminded him.

'So?'

'So I'm going to my own room.'

She had almost reached the door when his fingers closed around her wrist, stopping her. 'No, Sophia. I'd like you to stay.'

Knowing it was useless to struggle, she said coldly, 'I want to leave.'

'Not tonight. Tonight you should be right here and sleeping with me.'

Though he spoke quietly, there was a hint of persuasion in his voice that was so tempting. She was almost convinced he really wanted her.

But she couldn't allow herself to believe such fantasy, so she stuck to her guns. 'I don't want to sleep with you.'

'Very well,' he said patiently, 'I'll rephrase that…sleeping in the same bed.'

Sophia lowered her eyes. 'I don't want to sleep in your bed.'

He raised an eyebrow. 'You did last night.'

She flushed. 'That was a mistake, and I don't want to repeat it. I want to go back to my own suite.'

'After all I've gone through this evening, there's no way I'm letting you out of my sight.'

Then, as though the thin thread of his patience had snapped, he demanded, 'What in heaven's name made you run off and go wandering about on your own? Haven't you *any* sense?'

'You told me Venice was a safe city,' she said defensively.

'And so it is, except in very exceptional circumstances.'

Urging her back to her chair, he pressed her into it and said harshly, 'Dear God, have you no idea what you've put me through? When I came back and found you'd vanished into thin air... Then when we were out searching for you and I heard you scream—'

He bit off the words and, a white line appearing round his mouth, dropped into the chair opposite.

All at once, belatedly, she realized that he was furiously angry.

His reaction reminded her of a near accident that she'd witnessed earlier in the year.

A little boy had let go of his mother's hand and darted into the road almost under the wheels of a passing car. The driver had managed to do an emergency stop; then, getting out, he'd bundled the child back on to the pavement and into his mother's arms, before driving off.

Instead of comforting the boy, who'd been howling at the top of his voice, the distraught mother—having experienced the kind of fear that could only find an expression in anger—had shouted at him and shaken him, before starting to cry with relief.

Feeling the prick of tears behind her eyes, Sophia left her chair and, kneeling by Stephen's side, put her hand on his knee.

'I'm sorry...it didn't occur to me that you might be worried.'

His expression bleak, he said, 'It didn't occur to you that I might be worried! Do you seriously believe I think so little of you that I wouldn't care if harm came to you?'

She caught her breath. So he *did* care.

But the fact that he cared what happened to her didn't mean he loved her, she reminded herself sternly.

Even so, for the moment it was enough.

Worn out, physically and emotionally, she laid her head on his knee and felt his hand stroke her hair.

Then he was getting up and lifting her with him. 'Bed,' he said firmly. 'We'll sort out this mess in the morning.'

When, practically out on her feet, she swayed, he picked her up in his arms and carried her into the bedroom. Setting her down by the bed, he stripped off her robe and helped her in.

His own robe discarded, he stretched out beside her and gathered her close. Warm and safe in his arms, her head pillowed on his shoulder, she was asleep within seconds.

At first she slept the deep sleep of complete exhaustion, then, towards dawn, as her unconscious mind became enveloped in a miasma of intangible problems and disembodied terrors, her slumbers became disturbed and restless.

She found herself alone in the darkness. But she wasn't alone… She was being stalked by something malignant, something that meant to harm her.

Panic-stricken, she broke into a run, trying to outstrip it, but, in spite of all her effort, it was gaining on her, getting closer…

She awoke with a jolt, her heart racing and sobbing for breath. Though she was lying close by Stephen's side, his grip had relaxed with sleep and he was no longer holding her.

Needing the comforting warmth and reassurance his touch offered, she snuggled against him.

He was instantly awake and his arms closed around her, cradling her to him.

Feeling the tension in her slender body, he asked, 'What's wrong? Bad dreams?'

Her face buried against his neck, she nodded.

'Would you like a warm drink to help you relax? Milk? Hot chocolate?'

'No… Don't leave me.'

'I won't leave you.' Then, gently, 'It's still very early. Try to relax and get some more sleep.'

But it was impossible. Her brain had stirred into life and was active now, thoughts and images racing through her mind.

She recalled the Marquise's face as she'd said, 'Stefano is

mine… I am the one he loves, the one he intends to marry…if a cheap little slut chooses to throw herself at him, who can blame him for accepting what is offered…?'

Well, he might have looked on what happened the night before as simply taking a willing woman to bed, but he wasn't totally heartless. At least he'd cared enough to be concerned about her, to be angry and afraid when she had vanished.

But that didn't alter the fact that he intended to make another woman his wife.

Well, as soon as they had talked, had 'sorted out the mess' she would go back to London and leave him to marry the woman he was committed to.

But just for the moment *she* was here in his bed, lying in his arms. Just for the moment he was *hers*. If she was brave enough to bury her inhibitions, brave enough to risk a rebuff, she could maybe have just one more memory to take with her. One more precious memory to last her for the rest of her life.

'Stephen…'

He lifted a hand and brushed a tendril of hair away from her cheek. 'What is it?'

Summoning all her courage, she whispered, 'Will you make love to me?'

'Why?'

Floored by the question, she stammered, 'B-because I-I want you to.'

His voice cool, he said, 'You didn't seem to want that earlier.'

When she stayed silent, he asked, 'Or were you just playing games? Saying no because you enjoy using your power, enjoy keeping a man on a string?'

Aghast, she pulled free and, moving away, cried, 'How can you think that?'

Propping himself on one elbow so he could look down at her in the soft, pearly light of dawn, he demanded, 'What else am I to think? At dinner you showed every sign of being willing, not to say eager, to sleep with me. Then, by the time we'd had coffee you'd changed your mind. You didn't even want to share my bed...'

'I *did* want to, but—'

He laughed harshly. 'Oh, yes, so much so that you referred to making love with me as being *used*...'

'I only said that because I was upset. I didn't—'

'Don't try to tell me you didn't mean it. The mere thought was enough to send you running off into the night to escape such a fate...'

Seared by his bitterness, she said quietly, 'I'm sorry... Only you see when the Marquise told me that you loved her and that you and she were going to be married, I-I'm afraid I didn't altogether believe her. I thought it might be just wishful thinking on her part...' Sophia swiped a tear away, determined not to cry. 'Then, when you told me yourself that you were hoping to be married and that you had someone special in mind, well, I...I didn't want to sleep with another woman's man...'

'So that was all it was.'

'All?' she cried.

He looked amused by her indignation.

Flushing a little, she said, 'I'm sorry I'm not the kind of worldly, sophisticated woman who wouldn't care a jot—'

'*I'm* not,' he broke in crisply.

Then, his voice growing warmer, more intimate, he said softly, 'But we're wasting time. Do you still want me to make love to you?'

She half shook her head. 'I'm sorry; I shouldn't have asked you.'

'Why did you?'

After a moment's hesitation, she spoke the exact truth. 'I've decided to go back to London as soon as possible and I just wanted a final memory to take away with me.'

'I see.' His voice silky, he added, 'Then allow me to supply it.'

'No, really… As I said, I shouldn't have asked.'

'Of course you should have asked. I'm entirely at your service…'

There was something in his voice, a hint of hidden anger, that sent a little quiver running through her.

She desperately wanted him, wanted him to make love to her, but did she want it like this? She was so confused. She quivered. As he ran a hand down her slender body, she could feel herself give away to his caress. She couldn't help herself.

His palm lying warm at the base of her stomach, he smiled selfishly. 'This will drive the bad dreams away.'

'Please, Stephen…' Her voice trembled. How could she want him so much when she knew he didn't love her, was angry with her?

'Just relax and enjoy what I'm going to do to you.' He watched her face while his long fingers explored the smooth skin of her inner thighs and the silky nest of curls, before moving on to probe with delicate precision.

Feeling her shudder in response, he bent his head and took a pink nipple in his mouth…

For the next few minutes it was like riding a roller coaster, both frightening and exhilarating, as sensation followed sensation thick and fast.

Each time, when she thought she could feel no more, he wrung new sensations from her. Only when she was totally limp, a quivering mass of nerve-endings, did he show any mercy.

She couldn't deny that he had given her intense and prolonged pleasure, but it wasn't how she had wanted it to be.

Rather than this skill, this ability to rule her body and make it respond to his touch, she had wanted the warmth of *shared* love, wanted to feel his weight, wanted to take with her the memory of them reaching the heights together…

Tears squeezed themselves from beneath her closed lids and began to trickle down her cheeks.

He made a little inarticulate sound, then, whispering, 'Don't cry, my love, please, don't cry…' he began to kiss them away. 'I'm sorry, I've been such a brute to you.'

His tenderness only made her cry harder.

After a moment he gathered her close and held her, murmuring words of comfort while he stroked her hair.

When the tears finally stopped flowing, he said, 'I promise I won't touch you again.'

Her damp face against his throat, she muttered despairingly, 'But I *want* you to. I want you to make love to me properly.'

'You're sure about that?'

Knowing this was her last chance, and throwing pride to the winds, she said, 'Yes, I'm quite sure.'

Sated, she hadn't expected to feel anything other than the comfort and warmth of his body, but within a short space of time he had effortlessly rekindled her desire.

A desire that, with a combination of gentleness and passion, he then appeased, leaving her limp and quivering and, for the moment at least, utterly content.

With his fair head lying heavy on her breast, his breathing and the beat of his heart at one with hers, she was asleep within seconds.

She slept deeply, dreamlessly, and only awakened when the sun had scaled the wall and was slanting obliquely through the windows. Her watch showed it was almost eleven o'clock, and once again she was alone in the big bed.

Feeling oddly calm, tranquil, her mind in limbo, empty of thoughts, she got out of bed, and like an automaton, pulled on the discarded robe and went through to the adjoining bedroom.

Heading for the bathroom mechanically, she made the same mistake she had made the previous night and found herself in the dressing-room.

This time it was lit by sunshine, and she paused to glance around her. It was a pretty little room with a small blue-tiled fireplace, a chaise longue covered in rose-coloured velvet and a matching armchair.

Above the fireplace hung an oil painting. It was a portrait of a young woman with soft dark hair taken up into a mass of curls, dark eyes and a lovely heart-shaped face.

She wore a blue silk seventeenth century ball gown and a double rope of beautifully matched pearls which seemed to glow with an inner radiance—pearls that Sophia now recognized as the Padova Pearls. In her hand was a silver carnival mask.

For what seemed an age, Sophia stood staring up at it, completely stunned. It was undoubtedly the original from which her father had copied his miniature.

The miniature the Marquise had asked so many questions about and been so very eager to buy...

But Stephen had seen the miniature too, and if he had known this portrait was here, as surely he did, why hadn't he said something?

At length, having decided that the only way she would get an answer to the riddle was by asking him, she tore herself away and went to shower and put on some clothes.

When she was dressed in a cotton skirt and top, she took her hair up into a knot, pulled on a pair of flat sandals and, fascinated by the portrait, went to have another look at it.

She was still standing gazing up at it when Stephen's voice made her jump. 'So there you are! I was wondering where you'd got to.'

His tone held such relief that she knew he must have been

afraid that she had walked out once more, without waiting to talk to him.

She turned to see him standing in the open doorway dressed in olive-green trousers and a matching silk shirt open at the neck.

His handsome face looked a little tense, a little strained, as though it had become an effort to stay on top, and her heart went out to him.

'How are you feeling this morning?' he enquired, every inch the polite host.

With equal politeness, she answered, 'Very well, thank you.'

Then, returning her gaze to the picture, she asked flatly, 'When you saw the miniature at the gallery, why didn't you tell me about this portrait?'

'I wasn't sure whether you already knew of its existence and, if you didn't, it would have been too complicated to try and explain.

'You see, *I* didn't know about the miniature, and I was completely wrong-footed when Gina spotted it and made such a fuss about buying it.'

'But if you didn't know about the miniature, why did you come into the gallery?'

'To see you.'

'Oh…' Then, gathering herself, she asked, 'When the full-sized portrait was already here at the Palazzo, why was the Marquise so keen to have the miniature?'

'She wasn't aware that the full-sized portrait *was* still at the Palazzo.

'Because Paolo had taken a strong dislike to it, and in one of his drunken rages had threatened to destroy it, Aunt Fran asked Roberto to take it down and hide it.

'Then, though it went against the grain to lie, she told Paolo that it had been sold. It was only after his death that she had it moved into here.'

Puzzled, Sophia remarked, 'It seems strange that he should have taken such a strong dislike to a lovely old painting like this.'

'It isn't old. The dress and the hairstyle are misleading. If you were to examine it more closely you would see that it was painted about the same time as the miniature…'

As she glanced at him sharply, he added quietly, 'And by the same person.'

'You think Dad painted them both?'

'Undoubtedly.'

'Then how did it come to be here?'

'This was where it was painted. It's a portrait of Aunt Fran when she was young… She had held a fancy dress ball at the Palazzo for that year's *Carnevale* and she was wearing the dress she had had specially made for her…'

So her father had known that beautiful woman and hidden the fact, as Stephen had tried to hide it.

Aloud, she began, 'But if you knew that your aunt and my father had known each other, why didn't you——?'

She broke off abruptly as another realization struck her. 'Our meeting wasn't an accident,' she said with certainty.

'No.'

'You were following me.'

'Yes.'

'Why?'

He sighed. 'It's a long and complicated story which, in any case, I'd intended to tell you before you went back to London.

'However, as you must be feeling hungry, I suggest we have lunch first. Afterwards I'll tell you everything I know.'

It was another beautiful day and they ate their lunch—a seafood platter and a mixed salad, followed by fresh fruit and cheese—in the garden beneath the sun-dappled shade of a cool green canopy of leaves.

They ate in silence, a tension between them that had—

Sophia realized—as much to do with her decision to go back to London as with the story he had promised to tell her.

When they had finished the simple but delicious meal, Rosa cleared away and brought them coffee.

Settled in one of the comfortable loungers, Sophia watched Stephen fill two cups, before she prompted, 'You said that after lunch you'd tell me everything.'

He glanced up, his brilliant eyes narrowed against a shaft of sunlight. 'And so I will.'

Having handed her a cup, he sat down in the lounger alongside hers and added, 'I was just wondering where to start.'

'Start by telling me why the Marquise wanted the miniature so badly, when it was a portrait of a woman she frankly hated.'

'Gina wanted the miniature because Aunt Fran had been wearing the Padova Pearls.

'Shortly after that portrait was painted the pearls disappeared. My mother and father presumed they'd been transferred to the bank to prevent Paolo getting his hands on them.

'To the best of my, and the rest of the family's, knowledge they were never seen again.

'During her final illness, Aunt Fran had been in touch with her solicitor and made her last wishes known, but she failed to lodge her will with him, and it couldn't immediately be found.

'However, at her funeral, and following her precise instructions, her solicitor advised the family of her last wishes. Apart from a substantial legacy for Rosa and Roberto, the Palazzo and everything in it had been left to me, while the Padova Pearls she had bequeathed to her daughter.

'As she and Gina had never liked each other, that bequest came as both a surprise and a shock to the rest of the family.

'Gina was cock-a-hoop until it emerged that the pearls weren't with the bank and couldn't be found. It was almost as if they had never existed.

'Rosa and Roberto, the two people closest to Fran, denied all knowledge of them, and that portrait was the only tangible proof that she had ever had them.

'Gina practically accused Rosa and Roberto of stealing them, but they both stoutly denied knowing anything about their disappearance.

'My parents were of the opinion that if the pearls *had* been stolen the most likely person would have been Paolo.

'However, as he had remained here until his death, and Aunt Fran had never said anything about them being missing, I was inclined to believe that she herself had put them somewhere safe.'

'But they didn't come to light?' Sophia asked.

Stephen shook his head. 'Gina, having given up the idea that Rosa and Roberto had stolen them, began to think along the same lines as myself...

'To try and solve the mystery, I set about looking, but of course the Palazzo's a big place to search...'

When he fell silent, Sophia said, 'Speaking of the Palazzo, you were going to tell me how my father came to be here.'

CHAPTER TEN

As THOUGH wondering how to begin, Stephen reached to put both their coffee cups on the table, before saying abruptly, 'Fran had a childhood friend of whom she was very fond. This friend's name was Maria Caldoni...'

'My mother...' Sophia breathed.

'That's right. When the Caldoni family moved to Rome, the two girls missed each other very much, so after Maria and your father met and got engaged, whenever they could get away from Rome, they came to stay at the Palazzo.

'My parents and I were still living here, and though I could only have been about five and a half, I vaguely remember them coming...

'By this time, of course, Aunt Fran was married to Paolo and, though she soon realized that she had made a very bad mistake, she did her best to hide it from everyone.

'The following year, Maria and your father came for the carnival and it was then that he painted Fran's portrait and, I believe, the miniature for himself. He also began a portrait of my father...'

Her heart racing, Sophia said, 'So that's why it looks so much like you.'

'That's why... It remained unfinished because, not long afterwards, we moved to the States.'

Still marvelling, she said, 'I can't get over the likeness… It's incredible.'

'Though of course Dad's altered over the years, I know from photographs that when he was my age we looked very much alike. The main difference has always been in height. I'm several inches taller…'

'If you knew who it was when you saw the portrait, why didn't you tell me?'

'For the same reason I didn't tell you about the miniature. As I said, it's a long and complicated story, and I didn't know how much you already knew.

'It's only this last weekend—when I got round to reading the diaries Aunt Fran had left, and talked to Rosa—that I learnt the whole of it myself.'

Glancing at his companion's expressive face, he said wryly, 'Yes, I'm quite aware that reading someone else's diaries seems like prying, and I would never have opened them if Aunt Fran hadn't explicitly stated—in the will we finally found—that she had left them for me to read.

'She added that she wanted the people she loved best to know and understand what her life had been like and what had motivated her actions.'

Still a shade uncomfortable, Sophia asked, 'But would she have wanted *me* to know what was in them?'

'Yes,' he said with certainty, 'she would… Now, shall I go on?'

'Please.'

'It was after that particular carnival that Paolo got drunk and Aunt Fran discovered his real reason for marrying her…'

Watching Sophia's face, Stephen went on carefully, 'By that time, though your father was still very fond of Maria, he had fallen hopelessly in love with Fran and she with him…'

After a stunned silence, Sophia said incredulously, 'My father and your aunt loved each other?'

'Yes. Perhaps Paolo guessed and felt threatened, because he took a violent dislike to the portrait your father had painted.

'It wasn't long after that that the real break between Fran and Paolo occurred and Paolo took Gina and moved out of the Palazzo.

'When your father learnt that Paolo had left, he begged Fran to get a divorce and marry him. Though Maria's parents had planned a big society wedding and all the arrangements were in place, he was prepared to tell his bride-to-be and her parents the truth and cancel the wedding.

'But, much as she loved him, Fran wouldn't let him.

'As fate would have it, it was then that the Caldonis went to Cape Town for a month to visit a distant relative and took Maria with them.

'Your father arranged to have some leave of absence and .went to Venice alone to try to persuade Fran to change her mind. With their future happiness at stake, she must have been badly torn, but in the end she stayed firm.

'She said that she didn't believe in divorce and she refused to ruin her best friend's happiness. She told your father that she would always love him and if he really and truly loved her he would go ahead and marry Maria.

'He returned to Rome and, when Maria and her parents came back from South Africa, the marriage took place.

'What neither Fran nor your father knew at the time was that she was pregnant with his child.'

'After a couple of months, just as Fran realized she was pregnant, Paolo returned briefly to the Palazzo to see if his absence had changed her mind.

'In the circumstances she must have been tempted to say it had, and take him back, but once again she stuck with her principles.

'When he discovered that she still had no intention of including him in her will, he left again, apparently for good...'

As Sophia stared at him, struggling to take it all in, Stephen went on quietly, 'As soon as her pregnancy started to become obvious, Fran never left the Palazzo and, apart from Rosa and Roberto, only your father and Maria knew.

'But while your father knew the whole truth, Maria presumed that the baby was Paolo's.

'When Maria and your father had been married about three months and Maria became pregnant, they were both overjoyed. But, only a few weeks into the pregnancy, she had a miscarriage.

'Then, as a final death knell to their hopes, the doctor warned them that the bouts of rheumatic fever Maria had suffered as a child had weakened her heart and that another pregnancy might well kill her.

'She was willing to try, but your father wasn't, and when she realized that he was quite adamant she sank into a deep depression and lost the will to live so completely that he began to fear he would lose her anyway.

'Fran was desperately sorry for them both and, trying to make amends for the wrong she felt she'd done—both to her friend and the man she loved—she promised them that if the child she was carrying was born safe and well, they could adopt it.

'She made only two stipulations. The first was that no one, particularly Paolo, should ever know that she had borne a child. Perhaps she thought that if he found out she had had a baby he might guess the truth and try to make trouble. The second was that the child should never know that he or she had been adopted.

'Only too pleased to agree, the pair gave their word and, a week before the birth was due, they came to stay at the Palazzo.

'The adoption papers were all ready, just waiting to be filled in and signed, and with Fran's doctor and legal adviser—both sworn to secrecy—standing by, they waited on tenterhooks for the baby to be safely delivered…'

'And was it?' Sophia breathed, almost sure that the tale was going to end in tragedy.

But Stephen answered, 'Yes, it was. On the sixth of March—her own birthday—Fran had a little girl.'

Feeling as though she had been kicked in the solar plexus, Sophia said huskily, 'The sixth of March is *my* birthday.'

'Yes,' Stephen agreed quietly.

'So I'm *Fran's* daughter?'

'Yes. She was a very strong woman. Because of her principles she gave up not only the man she loved, but the daughter she had always wanted.'

'Maria and your father would have named you Francesca, but Fran suggested that you were called Sophia…her middle name.'

Through stiff lips, Sophia queried, 'And she never saw me again?'

'For Maria's sake, she never asked to. But when you were about four Maria herself insisted on bringing you to the Palazzo so Fran could see you.

'In my aunt's diary she states that those few days were the happiest of her life, and recalls how delighted you were when she scratched your name on a pane of glass with her diamond ring…

'So you see, the feeling that you'd been here before was really half forgotten memories.

'That was the last time she ever saw you, but she said she would always be thinking of you, and she intended to give you the Padova Pearls on your twenty-fifth birthday.

'Then as that birthday approached, almost as though she had had a premonition, the last entry in her diary said that she expected to be with her maker before then and was taking steps to ensure that the pearls reached you safely.

'She added that as neither Maria nor Paolo were still living and couldn't be hurt, she was giving your father permission to tell you the truth at the same time.

'Presumably, if he hadn't died when he did, you would have learnt the truth from his own lips rather than second hand.

'But it wasn't until Fran's will finally came to light that anyone here, apart from Rosa and Roberto, knew that she had a daughter of her own.

'In that will, it not only stated that she wanted her daughter to have the pearls, it actually *named* that daughter as Sophia Jordan.

'When Gina discovered that Fran had never intended her to have the pearls, she was furious. At first she refused to believe that any such daughter existed, and she swore that Fran had made the whole thing up just to spite her.

'But then Rosa and Roberto confirmed the fact that Fran did indeed have a daughter.

'The pearls still hadn't come to light, but they weren't the only thing that was missing. The jewellery box that Aunt Fran had had for as long as I can remember seemed to have vanished.

'When I asked Rosa about it, I discovered that, not long before she died, Fran had sent Roberto to London with a package—which Rosa presumed was the box—to give to your father—'

'Of course!' Sophia exclaimed.

Stephen lifted a level brow. 'You didn't see him?'

'No, but Mrs Caldwell did, and she described him to me. The first time I met Roberto it briefly crossed my mind that he fitted her description very well.

'She told me he was carrying a package, and later, when I started to put two and two together, I realized it must have been the jewellery box I'd found in Dad's bureau.

'There was a card with it that read: "For Sophia, with all my love. Have a very happy twenty-fifth birthday".

'Dad hadn't been able to get out for some time, so I thought it must have been ordered from a special delivery gift service…

'With my birth sign carved on the lid it seemed so perfect, so fitting…'

'Fran would be pleased you like it. It was one of her most treasured possessions. Her parents had given it to *her* on her twenty-fifth birthday, and as you and she were both Pisceans, it was appropriate.'

Sophia's eyes filled with tears.

'As she sent you the box, it seemed logical that the pearls were in it...'

Wiping the tears away, Sophia shook her head. 'But they weren't... I wonder what happened to them?'

'I only wish I knew. It's possible that your father, knowing how valuable they were, took them out of the box and put them somewhere safe, but I—'

'I've just thought of something!' Sophia exclaimed. 'They could have been stolen. The night we met, after you'd gone and while I was over at Mrs Caldwell's, I'm pretty sure someone searched the flat.

'For one thing, when I got back, the living-room curtains were closed and I'm certain they were open when I went across... Or almost certain,' she amended honestly. 'And I think someone went through the drawers in my bedroom. Though I can't imagine how they managed to get in without a—' She abruptly stopped speaking.

There was utter silence for a moment or two, then she accused shakily, 'It was you... *You* searched the flat... You kept my keys and went back. Then, before you left, you dropped them under the coffee table...'

'Yes,' he admitted.

'So you were in London because of the pearls... You were trying to get them back.'

'I was in London because of the pearls, but I wasn't trying to get them back.'

'Then what *were* you trying to do?'

'I was trying to make sure that if Fran *had* sent the pearls, they had gone to the right person.

'Don't forget this was *before* I'd read the diaries and I'd never heard of Sophia Jordan, so when Gina, having learnt of Roberto's visit to London, became convinced that some fraudulent deception had taken place, I was unable to reassure her.

'In fact I was forced to agree that if the pearls *had* been handed over in that casual way to some unknown man, the whole thing was decidedly risky.

'Roberto, who had been told to go to a certain address and give the package to a Signor Jordan, had merely carried out his orders with no means of checking that it was the right man he'd given it to—'

'But as Dad had once been a frequent guest at the Palazzo, surely Roberto would have recognized him?'

'The relevant word is *once*… It's over twenty years since your father was here, and while Rosa would almost certainly have known him, Roberto, who rarely came into contact with the guests, didn't. He admitted as much when I asked him.

'So, to be on the safe side, I decided to go to London and do some on-the-spot detective work.

'When Gina found out, she asked if she could come with me. For all her apparent sophistication she hates travelling alone, and Giovanni Longheni, an old friend who had been living in California for a number of years, was in London on business. She said it would be a good chance for them to meet up and spend some time together. Which they did.

'Left to my own devices, it didn't take me long to discover that Peter Jordan had died and that the woman Aunt Fran had claimed as her daughter, was working at A Volonté art gallery.' His eyes searched hers, making sure she understood his intentions.

'I had no idea what kind of woman you were, and I wanted to know for sure that Aunt Fran hadn't been duped into parting with the pearls.

'So, on Friday evening, while Gina dined with Giovanni, I went into A Volonté and got my first look at you.' Stephen stroked his hand down her cheek. 'I was knocked sideways. Those eyes and the shape of your face, that air of quiet strength, convinced me that, no matter how bizarre it seemed, you could well be Fran's daughter.

'But still I needed some proof, and I needed to find out exactly how much you knew and whether or not you had the pearls.' He sat back and paused for a moment, allowing her to take in everything he had said so far.

'In order to even start finding out those things, I had to get to know you, so when you left the gallery I followed you.

'I was wondering how best to go about meeting you when your carrier broke…

'Your first reaction when you saw me fazed me. You looked at me as if you already knew me, as if my face was familiar to you.

'It wasn't until you mentioned the portrait, and I actually saw it, that I realized why…' Stephen smiled. 'Though that portrait seemed to confirm your connection with Venice and the Palazzo, there were still a lot of questions to be answered.

'Then I noticed Aunt Fran's jewellery box… Though you told me it had been empty, I felt I had to check…'

Sophia continued for him. 'So you took my keys and when you were sure I was safely out of the way, you searched the flat.' She could hardly believe she was saying the words.

'I'm sorry. It's not something I'm proud of.' Wryly, he added, 'And you can tell from the mess I made of things that it wasn't in my line.'

'Presumably you didn't find the pearls?'

'I'm afraid not and, as I wasn't sure how best to proceed, I went back to my hotel to have dinner and think things over.

'In spite of the fact that you had the jewellery box, I was almost convinced that you knew nothing about the pearls or anything else to do with the Palazzo, for that matter.

'But I couldn't be *absolutely* sure. I needed to find some

way of getting to know you better, of getting to the bottom of the mystery.

'I couldn't stay in London—that afternoon some urgent business had cropped up that I needed to attend to in person— so I thought if I could persuade you to come to Venice…

'I spent half the night wondering how best to achieve that and by morning I'd managed to come up with a plan—'

Sophia gasped. 'You lied about selling the paintings!'

'No, that part was quite true. What *wasn't* true was that, Aunt Fran's expert having met with an accident, I needed your help.

'It's a fact that he met with an accident, but as the first viewing isn't for months yet there's plenty of time for him to recover.

'However, that fairly innocent deception did the trick and you agreed to come.

'Needless to say, Gina was horrified. She didn't want you anywhere near the Palazzo. For two reasons.

'Firstly, she was afraid that, rather than actually *sending* the pearls, Fran might have told you where to find them. And still unwilling to believe you *were* Fran's daughter, she didn't intend you to have them if she could help it.

'Secondly, she was jealous. Though I've always been fond of Gina, I have no illusions about her, and I was well aware that she had me lined up as husband number two.'

Wryly, he added, 'Having a rich husband *and* the pearls would have suited her just fine.

'So, you see, you were a threat to her…

'Her only slight consolation was that you had insisted on staying at a hotel.

'Then, when I got back to Venice on Saturday, I did what I should have done sooner. I read Aunt Fran's diaries. And of course they explained everything. Or almost everything…

'Gina was far from pleased to learn that the pearls were yours by right. She was even less pleased when, on Monday evening, she discovered that you were actually staying at the Palazzo. She wanted me to find you a hotel room without delay.

'But, having gone to a lot of trouble to make sure you *were* staying at the Palazzo, I had no intention of obliging her…'

Suddenly recalling the look that had passed between Stephen and the desk clerk, Sophia cried accusingly, 'The fact that I had no room… It was *your* doing!'

When, a gleam in his grey eyes, he failed to deny it, she rushed on, 'You suggested which hotel I should go to, then you bribed the clerk not to make a booking. Why?'

'Because I wanted you at my home, under my eye, so to speak, so I could assess the situation. However, there turned out to be some drawbacks to the plan.

'Rosa nearly gave the game away by first making it clear that you'd been *expected* at the Palazzo, and then by starting to mention your father.

'But it was Gina's opposition which proved to be the most serious. Until that intruder frightened you so badly, I'd failed to realize to what lengths she would go.'

'You mean the *Marquise* was behind that?'

He nodded sagely. 'Yes. I guessed when I realized that whoever it was must have had keys to the Palazzo. Gina still had her own set from when she had lived here, and she was the likeliest person to have given them to him…'

'But what was he *doing* in the Palazzo?'

'Looking for the pearls. He was told to search your belongings in case you had brought them with you, or managed to find them, but he hadn't completed his task when you went back to your suite.

'That was confirmed last night when Rosa came to tell me that Roberto needed to speak to me urgently.

'I found that a couple of the servants had cornered a man who was lurking in the garden, presumably waiting until it was dark before he let himself in.

'Unfortunately, by the time I got there he had managed to give them the slip and escape, but Roberto was able to identify him as one of the servants who work at Ca' d'Orsini.

'When I came back and couldn't find you, I was worried. But my anxiety was increased tenfold when one of the staff mentioned that he'd seen you slip out of the south entrance, and then Rosa told me about the threats she'd overheard Gina making.

'I couldn't believe she meant to do you any *real* harm, but I was scared stiff all the same…' He raked a hand through his hair.

'You hadn't taken your bag, so I knew you had no phone with you and no money to get a taxi to wherever you were intending to go. Which meant you were walking alone and at night with this man on the loose and probably still close by…

'I straight away organized a search party and set off myself to look for you.

'In the meantime my worst fears had been realized when our would-be intruder, who'd been spying on you and knew what you looked like, happened to see you leave the Palazzo.

'He reported as much to his mistress—they were keeping in touch by mobile phone. Seeing the perfect opportunity to scare you into leaving Venice, she gave him his instructions.'

Stephen's handsome face hardened. 'She didn't know anyone would be at hand to help, she didn't even know if you could swim, so telling him to push you into the canal was unforgivable.'

A kind of shudder shook him, before he said, 'I can only thank God that I was returning across the *campo* when I heard you scream. If I hadn't been there at that minute you could have drowned.

'First thing this morning I went to see Gina and told her—' He stopped speaking as Rosa approached with a tray of cool drinks.

Having put it on the table, she collected the coffee cups, then hesitated.

Glancing at her, Stephen asked, 'Something wrong?'

'Nothing's *wrong*, Signor Stefano, but when Roberto and I were talking just now, he happened to mention that when he was given the package to take to London there was a letter with it. I just thought you ought to know.'

'Thank you, Rosa.'

What she saw as her duty done, the housekeeper gave a little sigh of relief and departed.

'Of course,' Stephen said, 'I should have realized. Roberto only speaks a few words of English, so if Fran hadn't already phoned Peter and explained what her intentions were, there would have needed to be a letter…'

Accepting a tall frosted glass of fruit juice, Sophia took a sip and, anxious to know what he had said to the Marquise, prompted, 'You were saying you went to the Ca' d'Orsini…'

'Yes, I went to have it out with Gina. At first she denied all knowledge of the attack. Then, when I threatened to go to the police and tell them everything, she admitted that the man had been acting on her instructions. But she swore she'd never meant to harm you, only frighten you into leaving.

'At that point, perhaps in the hope of making me jealous, she told me that Giovanni Longheni, the old flame she met in London, had asked her to marry him and go back to California with him.

'He had given her a few days to think it over, and said if the answer was yes he would come and fetch her.

'Giovanni has loved her for years. I think I told you that when he was a young man he wanted to marry her. But his parents didn't like her and, though I believe she loved him as much as it's possible for her to love any man, she refused. She was afraid they would cut him off without a penny, and she couldn't stand the thought of being poor.

'However, it seems that after leaving college, Giovanni went into electronics and made a sizable fortune of his own, so money is no longer a problem.

'Even so, having set her sights on me and still cherishing hopes, she was reluctant to give him an answer, until I finally dashed those hopes by strongly advising her to accept his proposal.'

Her voice far from steady, Sophia began, 'You mean you're not…?'

'I mean I've never had the slightest intention of marrying Gina. Though, until now, I've always been fond of her, she's the last woman in the world that I'd want to spend my life with. She only told you all those lies to get rid of you.'

He took the glass from Sophia's nerveless fingers and, having deposited it on the table, raised her hand to his lips. 'I can understand why you felt used if you thought I was taking you to bed while all the time I was planning to marry her…'

'But *you* said you were hoping to be married.'

'I am, if you'll have me.'

'Me?' Sophia whispered.

'You're the woman I want to be my wife, my friend and my lover, my lifelong companion and the mother of my children. From the moment I saw you I was lost, head over heels in love. I couldn't imagine the rest of my life without you by my side…

'I'd started to hope and believe that you felt the same, but when you told me you'd decided to leave, I thought I'd been mistaken…'

She looked up and met his piercing gaze. 'Is that why you were angry?'

He nodded. 'I thought you didn't care.'

'I was leaving because I cared too much.'

'My precious darling…' Pulling her on to his lap, he began to kiss her. He kissed her until the whole world was spinning and nothing existed in the universe but him.

After a while he lifted his head to ask, 'How soon will you marry me?'

Her heart overflowing with joy and gladness, she told him, 'As soon as you like.'

That earned her another long kiss.

When at length he freed her lips, a quiver in her voice, she remarked, 'I wish Dad could have known how things have turned out. I'm sure he would have been happy for us.'

Stephen nodded. 'I believe Fran would have been too... I only wish we could find her pearls so you could wear them on your wedding day...'

Almost to himself he added, 'It's a great pity we don't know what was in Fran's letter; there might have been some clue...'

'Knowing Dad, he wouldn't have destroyed it,' Sophia said with certainty. 'It's probably still in his bureau. Apart from one or two documents I needed to find, I haven't gone through his papers...'

Then, her excitement rising, 'Old Mrs Caldwell has a key to the flat; what if I phone her and ask her to go across and look for it?'

'Yes, why not?' Stephen rose to his feet, taking Sophia with him. 'You've everything to gain and nothing to lose.'

On hearing Sophia's voice, Mrs Caldwell exclaimed, 'How lovely to hear from you, dearie!'

After asking the old lady how she was, and answering her first eager rush of questions, Sophia voiced her request, adding, 'Presumably, as it was hand delivered, it won't have a stamp, so if it *is* still there it should be fairly easy to pick out.'

'If you want to hang on, dearie, I'll go straight across and see if I can find it.'

The old lady was back quite quickly. Sounding a little breathless, she announced, 'I've found a letter that might be the one. The envelope just has your father's name on it. Would you like me to post it on to you, or shall I open it and read it out?'

After glancing at Stephen and getting his nod of approval, Sophia said, 'Will you read it out?'

'Certainly, dearie, if that's what you want.'

There was a rustle of paper; then, as both Sophia and Stephen listened, the old lady announced, 'It's quite short. It simply says:

'To my dearest. After all these years apart there's so much to say, yet nothing. You have my blessing to tell my darling Sophia the truth on her twenty-fifth birthday, and I'd like you to give her, on my behalf, the Padova Pearls and my jewellery box.

'For a long time now the box has kept my secret well. There's a little trick—move the tails of the seahorses in opposite directions.

'I love you and I always will. I feel I haven't got long on this earth, but love never dies and, God willing, we will meet again in some other place.

Francesca.'

Trying to bite back tears, Sophia thanked the old lady and, after promising to explain the whole thing before too long, rang off.

Quivering with excitement she went through to the bedroom and returned with the jewellery box. Standing it on the coffee table, she bent and, with her thumbs, pressed the tails of the tiny seahorses in opposite directions.

There was a faint click and the curved top of what she had supposed to be a solid lid sprang open.

Tucked into the space was a bag made of fine chamois leather. With unsteady hands, she opened the drawstring and drew out a double rope of lustrous pearls. 'They're beautiful,' she whispered in awe.

'Nowhere near as beautiful as you.'

As she half shook her head, Stephen took the pearls from her nerveless fingers and fastened them around her slender throat.

Then, drawing her into his bedroom, he locked the door behind them and closed the curtains.

'What are you doing?' she breathed.

Starting to strip off her clothes, he said, 'I have a fancy to make love to you while you're wearing nothing but the pearls…'

When she was completely naked, he took the pins from her hair and kissed her.

'But first I want you to see yourself as I see you…' He turned her to face the cheval-glass. 'There… How do you think you look?'

She saw a tall, slender-limbed woman with dark hair tumbling round her smooth golden shoulders and pearls glowing softly at her throat. On her face was a look of love that made her beautiful. 'I think—'

'And don't say half baked.'

'I wasn't going to.'

'What were you going to say?'

Thickly, she said, 'I think it's about time we were on an equal footing.'

Grinning, he invited, 'If you mean what I think you mean, go ahead.'

Turning, she unfastened the buttons of his shirt and pulled it free from his waistband. Then, fumbling a little, she undid the clasp of his trousers and slid down the zip.

Truth to tell, she had expected him to take over, but he stood with a slight smile on his chiselled lips, making no attempt to help.

Blushing furiously now, but determined not to be beaten, she slid first his trousers and then his silk boxer shorts down over his lean hips.

Having removed his own footwear, he straightened and said in her ear, 'If you're going to blush like this every time you try something new, married life is going to be a whole lot of fun.'

Then, drawing her back against his naked body, he turned them to face the mirror once more and, his hands cupping her breasts, his thumbs brushing lightly over the firming nipples, he watched her mouth soften and her eyes grow slumbrous as her body responded to his touch.

But this time, as she watched him, she saw that, rather than simply looking like a triumphant male, his handsome face reflected all the love in hers.

She smiled at him and he smiled back, before lifting her into the big four-poster and sliding in beside her.

HARLEQUIN *Presents*

The Rich, the Ruthless and the Really Handsome

How far will they go to win their wives?

A trilogy by Lynne Graham

Prince Rashad of Bakhar, heir to a desert kingdom;
Leonidas Pallis, scion of one of Greece's leading dynasties
and Sergio Torrente, an impossibly charismatic,
self-made Italian billionaire.

Three men blessed with power, wealth and looks—
what more can they need? Wives, that's what…and
they'll use whatever means to get them!

THE GREEK TYCOON'S
DEFIANT BRIDE
by Lynne Graham
Book #2700

Maribel was a shy virgin when she was bedded by impossibly
handsome Greek tycoon Leonidas Pallis. But when Maribel
conceives his child, Leonidas will claim her…as his bride!

**Don't miss the final installment of Lynne Graham's
dazzling trilogy! Available next month:**

THE ITALIAN BILLIONAIRE'S
PREGNANT BRIDE
Book #2707
www.eHarlequin.com

HP12700

QUEENS *of* R♥MANCE

The world's favorite romance writers

New and original novels you'll treasure forever from internationally bestselling Presents authors, such as:

Lynne Graham

Lucy Monroe

Penny Jordan

Miranda Lee

and many more.

Don't miss
THE GUARDIAN'S FORBIDDEN MISTRESS
by Miranda Lee
Book #2701

Look out for more titles from your favorite
Queens of Romance, coming soon!

www.eHarlequin.com

REQUEST YOUR FREE BOOKS!

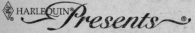

2 FREE NOVELS PLUS 2 FREE GIFTS!

YES! Please send me 2 FREE Harlequin Presents® novels and my 2 FREE gifts. After receiving them, if I don't wish to receive any more books, I can return the shipping statement marked "cancel." If I don't cancel, I will receive 6 brand-new novels every month and be billed just $3.80 per book in the U.S., or $4.47 per book in Canada, plus 25¢ shipping and handling per book and applicable taxes, if any*. That's a savings of close to 15% off the cover price! I understand that accepting the 2 free books and gifts places me under no obligation to buy anything. I can always return a shipment and cancel at any time. Even if I never buy another book from Harlequin, the two free books and gifts are mine to keep forever.

106 HDN EEXK 306 HDN EEXV

Name	(PLEASE PRINT)	
Address		Apt. #
City	State/Prov.	Zip/Postal Code

Signature (if under 18, a parent or guardian must sign)

Mail to the Harlequin Reader Service®:
IN U.S.A.: P.O. Box 1867, Buffalo, NY 14240-1867
IN CANADA: P.O. Box 609, Fort Erie, Ontario L2A 5X3

Not valid to current Harlequin Presents subscribers.

Want to try two free books from another line?
Call 1-800-873-8635 or visit www.morefreebooks.com.

* Terms and prices subject to change without notice. NY residents add applicable sales tax. Canadian residents will be charged applicable provincial taxes and GST. This offer is limited to one order per household. All orders subject to approval. Credit or debit balances in a customer's account(s) may be offset by any other outstanding balance owed by or to the customer. Please allow 4 to 6 weeks for delivery.

Your Privacy: Harlequin is committed to protecting your privacy. Our Privacy Policy is available online at www.eHarlequin.com or upon request from the Reader Service. From time to time we make our lists of customers available to reputable firms who may have a product or service of interest to you. If you would prefer we not share your name and address, please check here. ☐

HP07

THE ROYAL HOUSE OF NIROLI

Always passionate, always proud.

**The richest royal family in the world—
a family united by blood and passion,
torn apart by deceit and desire.**

By royal decree Harlequin Presents is delighted to bring you
The Royal House of Niroli. Step into the glamorous, enticing
world of the Nirolian Royal Family. As the king ails he must
find an heir.... Each month an exciting new installment
follows the epic search for the true Nirolian king. Eight heirs,
eight passionate romances, eight fantastic stories!

A ROYAL BRIDE
AT THE SHEIKH'S
COMMAND
by Penny Jordan
Book #2699

A desert prince makes his claim to the
Niroli crown.... But to Natalia Carini
Sheikh Kadir is an invader—he's already
taken Niroli, now he's demanding her
as his bride!

HARLEQUIN® *Presents*®

Harlequin Presents would like to introduce brand-new author

Christina Hollis

and her fabulous debut novel—

ONE NIGHT IN HIS BED!

Sienna, penniless and widowed, has caught the eye of the one man who can save her—Italian tycoon Garett Lazlo. But Sienna must give herself to him totally, for one night of unsurpassable passion....

Book #2706

Look out for more titles by Christina, coming soon—only from Harlequin Presents!

www.eHarlequin.com

HP12706